LET'S CLAP, JUMP, SING & SHOUT; DANCE, SPIN & TURN IT OUT!

ALSO BY PATRICIA C. McKISSACK

For older readers

Never Forgotten

Porch Lies: Tales of Slicksters, Tricksters, and Other Wily Characters

The Dark-Thirty: Southern Tales of the Supernatural

For younger readers

The All-I'll-Ever-Want Christmas Doll

Mirandy and Brother Wind

A Million Fish . . . More or Less

Stitchin' and Pullin': A Gee's Bend Quilt

LET'S CLAP, JUMP, SING & SHOUT;
DANCE, SPIN & TURN IT OUT!

Games, Songs & Stories from an African American Childhood

collected by PATRICIA C. McKISSACK

illustrated by BRIAN PINKNEY

schwartz & wade books · new york

Library of Congress Cataloging-in-Publication Data
Names: McKissack, Pat, author. | Pinkney, J. Brian, illustrator.
Title: Let's clap, jump, sing, and shout; dance, spin, and turn it out! : games, songs, and stories from an African
American childhood / collected by Patricia C. McKissack ; illustrated by Brian Pinkney.
Description: New York : Schwartz & Wade Books, 2017. | Includes bibliographical references.
Identifiers: LCCN 2016000969 (print) | LCCN 2016020086 (ebook) | ISBN 978-0-375-87088-0
ISBN 978-0-375-97088-7 (glb) | ISBN 978-0-307-97495-2 (ebk)
Subjects: LCSH: African Americans—Social life and customs—Juvenile literature. | African Americans—
Games—Juvenile literature. | African Americans—Songs and music—Juvenile literature. | African American
children—Juvenile literature.
Classification: LCC E185.86 .M424 2017 (print) | LCC E185.86 (ebook) | DDC 305.896/073—dc23

The text of this book is set in P22 Mackinac.
The illustrations were rendered in watercolor and India ink on Strathmore watercolor paper.
Book design by Rachael Cole

MANUFACTURED IN CHINA
2 4 6 8 10 9 7 5 3 1
First Edition

In memory of my beloved husband,
Fredrick L. McKissack, Sr., "Paw-Paw"
—P.C.M.

For my wife, Andrea, who brings me joy!
—B.P.

CONTENTS

A NOTE FROM THE ILLUSTRATOR

Creating the art for this book was pure joy. I drew on my memories of hearing these stories, songs, and rhymes as a child—in my Sunday school class at church, on the school playground at recess, and everywhere in between. I got quiet in my studio and listened to the memories. When I touched paintbrush to paper, the images danced from my hand onto the page.

Brian Pinkney
Brooklyn, New York

INTRODUCTION

Our earliest toys are our hands, feet, and voices. When we are babies, our wiggling fingers, curling toes, kicking legs, and flexing fists, combined with our squeals of wonder and surprise, provide us with hours of challenging and entertaining play while helping us develop basic learning skills.

Long before we have full command of language or any formal education, we can enjoy the rhythms and repetition of singsong rhymes that tell our fingers to become an "Itsy-Bitsy Spider" or our toes to become "This Little Piggy"—all-time favorites of children from many cultures.

As we grow, our play changes. Simple clapping games advance into more complicated body moves; we learn to skip, run, and jump rope. Games and songs performed in a circle are coupled with word games. Soon we start shaping whole stories, which we share with our family and friends. From singing simple songs of praise in Sunday school, we move to singing on the porch with our friends and join school and community choirs.

When I was young, like other children, I didn't understand that my play activities were an essential part of my growth and development. Though I never realized it, we were learning practical lessons, like how to count, the names of the states, the seasons, the days of the week, and the months of the year, as well as establishing our moral center regarding how to treat others fairly and honestly. Our teachers, pastors, counselors, and parents understood that even the most uncomplicated rhyme and rhythm games are educational tools that enhance creativity and develop decision-making and problem-solving abilities. We were encouraged to take part in these simple folk expressions and to teach them to our younger brothers and sisters and our classmates, as has been done for centuries.

In addition to their developmental and educational benefits, storytelling, wordplay, and games have helped expose generations of African American children to folk characters and historical figures, all of which have provided a connecting thread among people of color throughout the world.

Some of this material originated in Africa, or among early African American captives in the United States and the Caribbean—but others are not African in origin. Through the years, black children have learned games and folktales from other cultures, and have then made them uniquely their own by adding Afro-Caribbean rhythms and movements and by changing lyrics. Like all folk expressions, they have continually morphed over the years, and continue to do so today.

In writing this book, I have relied heavily upon my own play experiences as a child growing up in Kirkwood, Missouri, and Nashville, Tennessee, in the 1950s, and as a student, a teacher, an instructor of teachers, a parent and grandparent, and, finally, a writer. This really is a collection of my favorite childhood games, songs, poetry, and stories that are directly linked to my African American heritage.

What I remember best is how much fun I had making memories with my friends during our playtime. I hope you'll have just as much fun as you explore this book.

Patricia C. McKissack
St. Louis, Missouri

Chapter 1
FROM HAND TO HAND
HAND CLAPS

Hand clapping—one of the first forms of children's play—has been around for centuries, as have hand clapping rhymes. Like other groups who settled in the New World, African Americans swapped their hand claps with Native Americans and Europeans, and in this way, the beloved games passed from household to household, from culture to culture. Today many of them are global favorites, enjoyed by millions of children.

I shared these early rhymes with my classmates and neighbors on the playground of Turner School in Kirkwood, Missouri, and on my grandmother's porch in Nashville, Tennessee. Later, I taught my own children and grandchildren the hand claps, just as my mother and grandmother had shared them with me.

PATTY-CAKE

Over the centuries the "Patty-Cake" rhyme has changed and evolved, until now there are more than thirty variations of this beloved hand clap. One version dates back to the eighteenth century. It is believed that slave owners taught their slave babysitters the "Patty-Cake" rhyme so that the slaves could play with the children who lived in the Big House. Slave mothers adapted it for their own little ones by adding African rhythms and movements. Then the slaves passed on their version, and each generation made changes. This is the version that is used most often in the African American community today.

Patty-cake, patty-cake, baker man.

Make me a cake as fast as you can.

Roll 'em over, roll 'em over; put him in the pan.

Then bake 'em in the oven, Mr. Patty-Cake man.

MARY MACK

"Mary Mack" is one of the most popular hand clap rhymes in the English-speaking world. It was certainly one of my favorites. As with other hand claps, my friends and I adapted it, making changes to the rhythms, adding complicated hand movements, and upping the tempo to create a sassy performance.

Oh, Mary Mack, Mack, Mack,

All dressed in black, black, black,

With silver buttons, buttons, buttons,

Up and down her back, back, back.

She asked her mama, mama, mama,

For fifteen cents, cents, cents,

To see the elephant, elephant, elephant,

Jump the fence, fence, fence.

He jumped so high, high, high,

He touched the sky, sky, sky,

And never came back, back, back,

Till the Fourth of July, -ly, -ly!

SOLOMON GRUNDY

This nursery rhyme has been around since the nineteenth century.

In 1944, Alfred Bester and Paul Reinman introduced a comic-book character—a large zombielike archvillain—they named after the character in the rhyme. Solomon Grundy was an adversary of the Green Lantern, and later of Batman and Superman.

African American children transformed ol' Grundy yet again into a hand clap, and I remember sharing it with my first-grade friends. We performed it in a quick and spicy rhythm with lots of arm and leg movements.

Solomon Grundy,

Born on Monday,

Christened on Tuesday,

Married on Wednesday,

Took sick on Thursday,

Worse on Friday,

Died on Saturday,

Buried on Sunday.

So goes the ordinary life of

Solomon Grundy.

(Repeat, faster and faster each time.)

MONKEY HAND CLAPS

These hand claps first appeared during the great black migration from the South to the North around 1919, and became popular in New York City's Harlem in the 1920s. Southern children who moved north mixed and matched verses with their new neighbors, and soon a series of unique hand claps emerged.

Version 1 *(circa 1920)*

Monkey, monkey, monkey,

Swinging from a piece of thread.

The string broke; it aine no joke,

'Cause the silly little monkey's dead.

Version 2 (*circa 1930*)

There was a time,

When the goose drank wine,

And the monkey played the fiddle

On the streetcar line.

The line broke,

And the monkey got choked,

And the goose played the trumpet

On the Midtown Line.

Version 3 *(circa 1940–50)*

Once upon a time,

The goose drank wine,

And the monkey smoked a pipe

On the L&N line.

The train crashed,

And the monkey got smashed,

And the goose croaked taps

On the streetcar line.

Version 4 *(circa 1990)*
Sometimes "gorilla" is used in place of "monkey."

Great big monkey

Sitting on a fence,

Tryin' to make a dollar

Out of fifteen cents.

The fence broke,

That's all she wrote,

Singing sweet treat, sweet treat,

Sweet treat, twiddle dee-dee.

EENIE MEENIE MINEY MO

The "Eenie Meenie" hand claps are centuries old, with German, Welsh, English, and American roots. Originally, the rhymes were used to choose an "it" or to count a player in or out.

Around 1888, American schoolchildren began using a racial pejorative in the original rhyme. Black children, including my peers and I, dropped the offensive version, but we kept the basic wording and reshaped the rhyme into hand claps that were acceptable and distinctly our own. What follows is the original version as I first learned it.

Eenie meenie miney mo.

Catch a monkey (tiger, gremlin, zebra, etc.) by the toe.

If he hollers let him go.

Eenie meenie miney mo.

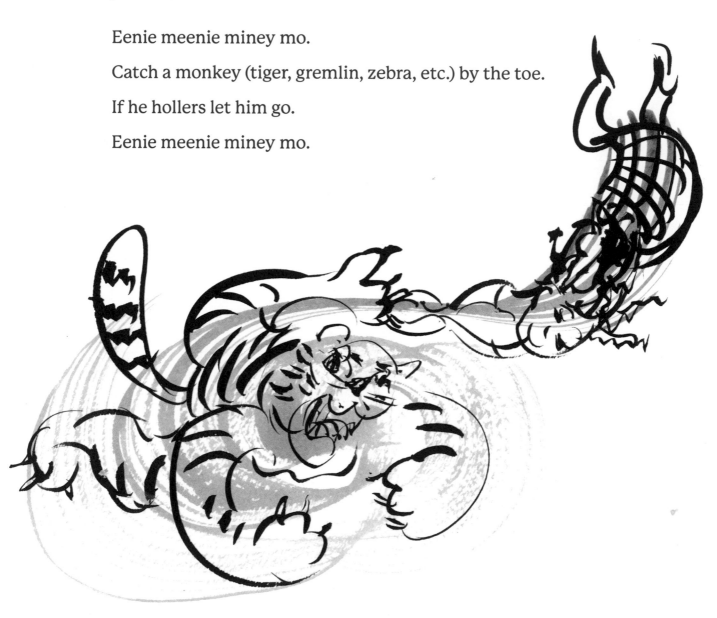

OTHER VERSIONS OF "EENIE MEENIE"

Henry Bolton Version

*This nineteenth-century version was first written down by Henry Bolton in 1888
and seems to be the origin of the African American adaptation that follows it.*

Eenie, meenie, tipsy, toe;

Olla, bolla, domino;

Okka, pocha, dominocha;

Hy, pon, tush.

African American Version

Eenie, meenie, tip 'n' teenie,

Apple Jack, John, and Sweeney.

Hochie, pochie, diamond nochie,

Hound, pound, touch.

EENIE MEENIE SASSAFREENY

This hand clap was inspired by "Eenie Meenie Miney Mo." Its origin can be traced to the rural South—Arkansas, Tennessee, Louisiana, Mississippi, Georgia, and Florida—where it first appeared in the early 1960s before spreading across the country. After I was introduced to it by my sister, Sarah, we performed the rhyme as fast as we could, making it a tongue twister.

Eenie meenie sassafreeny,

Oops ah thumbalini,

Achi cachi Liberace,

I love you.

Got a peach? Got a plum?

Got a stick of bubble gum?

Eenie meenie sassafreeny,

Oops ah thumbalini,

Say, you got no peach and got no plum.

All you've got is chewed-up gum!

Since you came with nothing to share,

We know just what to do.

Sing! Achi cachi Liberace,

I love you.

SHAME

When I was growing up during the 1950s, the southern United States was mostly segregated. There were many public places in Nashville where I couldn't go. We black children did this hand clap to poke fun at the stores whose rules restricted us.

Even if I could,

Oh, I'd never go to _____ *(Add the name of the place)*

Anymore, -more, -more.

There's a big floor walker

At the door, door, door.

He'll grab you by the collar,

And he'll make you scream and holler.

Oh, I'll never go to _____

Anymore, -more, -more.

SHIMMY, SHIMMY COCO POP

Very often we made up hand claps based on popular songs. For example, Little Anthony and the Imperials, an R&B vocal group, scored a hit in 1960 with "Shimmy Shimmy Ko-Ko Bop." It inspired this new hand clap rhyme, which spread across black communities from coast to coast. When I played it, my friends and I made up our own words, but we used Little Anthony's basic rhythm.

Down, down, baby, down by the roller coaster.

Sweet, sweet baby, I'll never let you go.

Shimmy, shimmy coco pop, shimmy, shimmy pow.

Shimmy, shimmy coco pop, shimmy, shimmy pow.

Grandma, grandma, sick in bed.

She called the doctor and the doctor said:

Let's get the rhythm of the head—ding dong!
(Move your head from left to right.)

Let's get the rhythm of the head—ding dong!
(Move your head from left to right.)

Let's get the rhythm of the hands.
(Clap twice.)

Let's get the rhythm of the hands.
(Clap twice.)

Let's get the rhythm of the feet.
(Stomp twice.)

Let's get the rhythm of the feet.
(Stomp twice.)

Let's get the rhythm of the hot dog.
(Shake your hips.)

Let's get the rhythm of the hot dog.
(Shake your hips.)

Put it all together and what do you get?

Shimmy, shimmy coco pop,

Shimmy, shimmy pow.

Shimmy, shimmy coco pop,

Shimmy, shimmy pow!

Chapter 2

TURN ABOUT
JUMP ROPE RHYMES AND GAMES

Jumping rope is ancient. The Egyptians, Greeks, and Romans used rope jumping for military training, athletic competition, and exercise, and just for fun, as we do today.

Jumping rope in the African American community is a matter of personal style, ability, and endurance. Some children are expert rope turners, while others are skilled athletic jumpers. Turners and jumpers from the same school or neighborhood often team up to create routines that are individualized and highly competitive. Teams compete in jumprope tournaments all over the globe.

My mother gave me a measure of clothesline to use as my first jump rope. As a solo jumper, I turned to the rhythm of a song, or sometimes counted to see how long I could go without missing. Some of my most memorable playtimes were when we'd use our rope to play different games, such as limbo and tug-of-war. I enjoyed being on the playground, matching my skills against other friends. My wish is that you will jump for joy, too!

SINGLE-ROPE JUMPING RHYMES

When and where single-rope jumping started is not known, but the rhymes are myriad and found throughout the world. Here are a few I remember.

ICE CREAM

Ice cream, ice cream,

Cherry on top.

How many boyfriends (girlfriends)

Have you got?

One, two, three . . .
(Jump until you miss.)

ONE TO TEN AND THEN AGAIN

One, two, buckle my shoe.

Three, four, shut the door.

Five, six, pick up sticks.

Seven, eight, open the gate.

Nine, ten, a big fat hen.

(Repeat.)

FOUND A DOLLAR

I found a dollar,

So what do I have?

Two half dollars.
(Jump twice.)

Four quarters.
(Jump four times.)

Ten dimes.
(Jump ten times.)

Twenty nickels.
(Jump twenty times.)

And a hundred pennies.
(Jump a hundred times.)

LETTERS

Early in the morning about eight o'clock,

What do I hear but the postman's knock?

Up jumps _____ *(your name)* to open the door,

And all the letters fall on the floor.

Let's count them: one, two, three, four . . .
(Jump until you miss.)

MISS MOUSEY

Although the origin of the Miss Mousey jumping rhymes is unknown, there is some evidence that they first appeared during slavery times. Miss Mousey sometimes becomes Miss Lucy, Miss Liza, Miss Fannie, or Aunt Sookie. "Miss Mousey" was one of my favorite rhymes, and I could solo-jump it or share it with others and have just as much fun.

Version 1

Miss Mousey, Miss Mousey, wee and smart,

Tell us the name of your sweetheart.
(Jump on each letter of the alphabet, A through Z, until you miss. The letter you miss on represents the first letter of your sweetheart's name.)

Version 2

Miss Lucy, Miss Lucy, wild and free,

Tell us the month your wedding will be.
(Jump on each month of the year in order. Add years at the end of each twelve months, and repeat until you miss.)

Version 3

Miss Fannie, Miss Fannie, please tell me,

How many children will there be?
(Jump on every number from 1 to 100 or until you miss.)

Version 4

Aunt Sookie's living.

Where's she living?

She settled in a place called Ten-nes-see.

She wed a man from Ken-tuc-ky.

Add their babies—one, two, three.

And now they're a happy family.
(Jump to 100, counting by twos, fives, or tens, while the rope turns faster and faster.)

23

HOT PEPPER

Hot pepper, or jumping rope as fast as you can, has been a part of rope turning and jumping for decades. It can be traced to the Northeastern urban centers of Boston, New York, and Philadelphia during the early twentieth century. Today, hot pepper routines are included in gymnastics, bodybuilding, and other exercise programs.

Hot pepper is always a challenge between the jumper and the turners. Can the jumper keep up with the fast-whipping rope? As a child, I tried but never lasted more than a few seconds!

Here are some rhymes that children use to set up the hot pepper jumping that comes at the end.

SET THE TABLE

_____, _____, *(Say your name twice.)*

Set the table

Just as fast as you are able.

Don't forget the salt and sugar

Or the spicy, red-hot pepper!
(The rope turners gradually increase the speed.)

HOT, HOT PEPPER

There's a girl who lives 'cross town

Who can set the city streets on fire

Jumping hot, hot pepper for hours.

Yes, it's true! I aine no liar. *(said with attitude)*

Let me show you how she does it.
(The rope turners gradually increase the speed.)

DOUBLE DUTCH

Double Dutch is a style of jumping performed with two ropes turning, eggbeater fashion, at the same time. The double Dutch rhymes that the rope turners chant tell the jumper or jumpers what to do. Older or more experienced jumpers often jump double Dutch.

JUMP WITH ME
(A single jumper begins the rhyme.)
I like coffee.

My friend likes tea.

I'd like for _____ *(name of another jumper)*

To jump with me.
(The jumper who has been named jumps in. The two jump hot pepper.)

25

PUTTIN' LI'L SISTER TO BED

Can you do what I tell you?

Turn around.

Touch the ground.

Wiggle your nose.

Touch your toes.

Climb the stairs.

Say your prayers.

Turn out the light.

Say goodnight.

I KNOW
(Begin with three jumpers.)
I know something,

But I won't tell:

Three little monkeys

In a peanut shell.

One can read.
(One jumper leaps out.)

One can dance.
(The second jumper leaps out.)

And one has a hole

In the seat of his pants.
(The third jumper leaps out.)

LEFT, RIGHT, LEFT
Peanut butter sandwich,

Made with bread and jelly,

Stick with us, we'll cheer you up, really.

Come on, _____, *(The jumper names someone. Let's call her Jo.)*

Jump in.

I can't! *(says Jo, who doesn't jump in)*

Why not?

I can't! *(says Jo)*

Why not?

My back's too sore, *(says Jo)*

My belt's too tight,

My body shakes from left to right.

Come on, Jo *(Jo jumps in now.)*

Jump. Jump.

Jump to the left,

To the right,

To the left, right, left.

To the left,

To the right,

To the left, right, left.

JUMP BACK, HONEY, JUMP BACK

After its publication in 1896, Paul Laurence Dunbar's poem "A Negro Love Song" became a double Dutch jump rope favorite among African American children, renamed "Jump Back, Honey, Jump Back." I remember lining up to leap in and out when this refrain was repeated. My fellow jumpers and I tried to jump through the whole poem without missing, but we seldom made it.

It was years later, when I was a teacher, that I learned the history of how Dunbar came to write his famous poem. During the Chicago World's Fair, in 1893, the young poet worked as a waiter in a restaurant. The poet's ears were always open, and the restaurant—busy and noisy—was a constant source of good story material. The cooks and waiters often talked about their dates and sweethearts.

One door connected the kitchen to the main dining area. Sometimes the waiters reached the door at the same time and crashed into each other. To avoid such accidents, the waiters yelled out a warning to whoever might be on the other side: "Jump back, honey, jump back." Hearing the rhythms of the restaurant all day, Dunbar wove the words into one of his most endearing poems.

Seen my lady home las' night,

      Jump back, honey, jump back.

Hel' huh han' an' sque'z it tight,

      Jump back, honey, jump back.

Hyeahd huh sigh a little sigh,

Seen a light gleam f'om huh eye,

An' a smile go flittin' by—

      Jump back, honey, jump back.

Hyeahd de win' blow thoo de pine,

      Jump back, honey, jump back.

Mockin'-bird was singin' fine,

      Jump back, honey, jump back.

An' my hea't was beatin' so,

When I reached my lady's do',

Dat I couldn't ba' to go—

      Jump back, honey, jump back.

Put my ahm aroun' huh wais',

      Jump back, honey, jump back.

Raised huh lips an' took a tase,

      Jump back, honey, jump back.

Love me, honey, love me true?

Love me well ez I love you?

An' she answe'd "'Cose I do"—

      Jump back, honey, jump back.

UNDER THE ROPE

Limbo, which we called Under the Rope, is based on a contest played on the Caribbean island of Trinidad, where players lean backward from the waist and shuffle under a pole called a limbo stick. Then the stick is lowered. The stick continues to be lowered until only one player can get under without using his or her hands to keep from falling on the ground. During the 1950s, when the game became popular in the United States, we used our jump ropes, held taut, to make a limbo stick, and recited this rhyme.

How low can you go, Smoky Joe?

How low can you go, Cindy Lou?

Limbo yes, limbo no.

Come along, here's what you do.

Limbo lower, no?

Limbo lower, yes?

Take it lower.

Lower, lower we go.

The best I've seen is Limbo Jean.

How far can you bend back, Limbo Jack?

Gotta be limber, gotta be quick,

If you wanna get under the limbo stick.

Take it lower now.

Lower still, pow!

Take my hand; we'll move as one.

And we'll limbo till the morning sun.

Take it lower now.

How low can *you* go?

TUG-OF-WAR

Tug-of-war has been a competitive game since the days of ancient Egypt and the pharaohs, and it is still enjoyed today by men, women, and children all over the world. In China, tug-of-war developed around the myth of the battle between Sun and Moon. During the twelfth century in India, rural communities had ceremonial tugs-of-war to see who was the strongest among them. And Native Americans used the game as a test of manhood and to settle disagreements. Africans arrived in the Colonies with knowledge of the sport. Plantation owners held tugs-of-war among their slaves and bet large sums of money on who would win.

   Tug-of-war is played much the way it was long ago in Africa, Asia, Europe, and the Americas. A line is drawn. Four to eight players divide into two teams. Each side takes hold of a long, strong rope and pulls it taut across the line on the ground. The object is for one team to pull the opposing team across the line.

I loved it when the boys competed against us girls. We always named our team after wild animals and were often the Pink Panthers. (We were thrilled when the movie was released in 1963, because that gave our name star quality.)

First, the referee yelled, "Get ready!" and the tension began to grow in my legs and arms. When he yelled, "I declare war!" our team tugged and tugged, trying to pull the boys over the line. Sometimes we won; sometimes we didn't. But the challenge was always fun.

This is the shout my friends and I made up to help us coordinate our pulls.

Pull that rope,

Uh-huh, uh-huh!

And don't dare flinch.

No, no, not once.

And don't give up—

Not one single inch.

Just pull that rope

With all your might,

And never give up.

Never, ever give up!

Till we win this fight,

Uh-huh! Uh-huh!

Now, pull that rope, huh!

Pull that rope, huh!

Pull that rope, huh!

Pull!

Chapter 3
SHAKE YO' BODY
CIRCLE GAMES AND RING SHOUTS

The Gullah people of the Sea Islands off the coasts of Georgia and South Carolina were originally slaves. Forbidden to have drums, they used their hands and feet to clap and stomp out African rhythms as part of religious rituals, moving in a counterclockwise circle. These ceremonies didn't include actual shouting at first. But by the nineteenth century, emotional outbursts of praise and joyful singing were added; thus the ceremonies became known as ring shouts. African American slave children took the idea of gathering in a circle from the adults and created their own play activities.

As a child, I was well acquainted with ring games. My friends and I would form a circle; then we'd choose a ring leader, who decided which song, game, or dance the group would play.

IF YOU'RE HAPPY

In the South after the Civil War, former slave children were encouraged to join in the celebration of their freedom, and they shared ring shouts that were lively and full of spirit. The following is an example of a popular chant from that time. It is still enjoyed by children of all ethnicities today, who perform the actions described as they're chanted. It became a favorite of mine after I learned it at the Phyllis Wheatley YWCA, in St. Louis Missouri, in 1955.

If you're happy and you know it, clap your hands.
(Clap twice.)

If you're happy and you know it, clap your hands.
(Clap twice.)

If you're happy and you know it, and you really want to show it,

If you're happy and you know it, clap your hands.
(Clap twice.)

If you're happy and you know it, stomp your feet.
(Stomp twice.)

If you're happy and you know it, stomp your feet.
(Stomp twice.)

If you're happy and you know it, and you really want to show it,

If you're happy and you know it, stomp your feet.
(Stomp twice.)

If you're happy and you know it, shout for joy. Hoo-ray!

If you're happy and you know it, shout for joy. Hoo-ray!

If you're happy and you know it, and you really want to show it,

If you're happy and you know it, shout for joy. Hoo-ray!

If you're happy and you know it, say Amen. A-men!

If you're happy and you know it, say Amen. A-men!

If you're happy and you know it, and you really want to show it,

If you're happy and you know it, say Amen. A-men!

If you're happy and you know it, do all four.
(Clap twice, stomp twice, shout "Hoo-ray! A-men!")

If you're happy and you know it, do all four.
(as above)

If you're happy and you know it, and you really want to show it,

If you're happy and you know it, do all four.
(as above)

LITTLE SALLY (WATERS) WALKER

This ring shout, which originated in the plantation South during the mid-nineteenth century, was first played by black and white children together. The black girls formed the outer circle, and the white girls stood in the center. After they all sang the chant, the groups exchanged places and repeated the verse.

After the Civil War, African American children changed Sally Waters to Sally Walker. In the early 1950s, when I was introduced to circle games, "Sally Walker" instantly became another one of my favorites. This is the way we played it: We formed a circle, then selected a ring leader to choose the player who would take the role of Sally Walker (or Jerry Walker if it was a boy). When I was chosen, I'd skip around the circle, miming the words with my hands on my hips. The best part was "letting my backbone slip."

Version 1: Plantation South *(circa 1850–1950)*

Little Sally Waters, sitting in a saucer,

Crying and weeping for a young man.

Rise, Sally, rise, wipe away your tears.

Look to the east,

Look to the west,

To find the one who is the best.

Version 2 *(circa 1950–80)*

Li'l Sally Walker, sitting in a saucer,

Rise, Sally, rise.

Wipe your weeping eyes,

Put your hands on your hips,

And let your backbone slip.

Shake it to the east,

Shake it to the west,

Shake it to the one you love the best.

Version 3 *(1980–present)*

Little Sally Walker, skipping down the street.

She don't know where she's going,

But she stopped in front of _____. *(The name should be the person Sally stops in front of. Let's use Lynn for an example.)*

(Sally does a short dance move, challenging the player.)
Hey, Lynn, hey, Lynn, can you do that move?

Can you move like that?

Come on, do that move, do that move,

Do that move for me.

(Lynn accepts the challenge by repeating the song and doing Sally's moves.)
Hey, Sally, hey, Sally, I can do that move.

I can move like that.

Come on, Sally, I can do that move,

Do that move like you.
(Then Lynn becomes the new Sally. And the game goes on.)

AUNT DINAH

"Aunt Dinah" ring shouts became popular during the last half of the nineteenth century, though their roots can be traced to slavery days. Older slaves were often referred to by whites as Aunt or Uncle, and white children would incorporate these titles into uncomplimentary songs or stereotypical stories about lazy or weak slaves.

It's not surprising that after slavery ended, blacks rejected these handles as a harsh reminder of the past and a time when former slave owners refused to address them respectfully. However, black children within the African American community were encouraged to use the terms. It was disrespectful for us to call our seniors by their first names, and using "Mr.," "Mrs.," and "Miss" sounded too formal. So we would use "Aunt" and "Uncle," with permission, as terms of endearment and respect. In time, the humiliation of these titles lessened, and now children of every race refer to family friends and neighbors as Aunt and Uncle.

Here's one of the ring shouts I enjoyed with my friends.

Aunt Dinah's Dead

Aunt Dinah's dead. *(ring leader)*

How'd she die? *(group)*

Oh, she died like this.
(ring leader, making an exaggerated gesture with body and face)

Oh, she died like that. *(group, trying to imitate the move)*

SHAKE YOUR BODY

When a friend called out "Shake your body," we'd quickly form a circle and respond, "Shake your body!" Then we'd sing our own words to the tune of a song made popular by calypso artist Harry Belafonte called "Jump in the Line (Shake, Señora)," trying to outdo each other with our calypso moves. Sometimes the ring leader called out the next move, such as "Twist," "Bend," or "Swing your body." Or perhaps the ring leader might point to a person in the circle, who'd call the next move. The idea was to be as creative as possible. The hardest command for me to follow was "Shake your eyes," because that meant I had to shake my head. That made me very dizzy, but even that was fun, stumbling around trying to keep my calypso balance. Here's the song we'd sing.

(The leader sings and demonstrates a move.)
Everybody,

Shake, shake, shake your body;

Shake your body light.

(The group sings and responds.)
Now shake, shake, shake your body;

Shake your body right.

Chorus: *(Everybody sings and does the move.)*

Jump in the line; shake your body in time.

Jump in the line; shake your body in time.

Jump in the line; shake your body in time.

'Cause shaking your body,

'Cause shaking your body,

Is not a crime.

(As before.)
Help me now,

Twist, twist, twist your body;

Twist your body light.

Twist, twist, twist your body;

Twist your body right.

(Chorus)
(As before.)

Hey there,

Bend, bend, bend your body;

Bend your body light.

Bend, bend, bend your body;

Bend your body right.

(Chorus)

(As before.)

Here we go now,

Work, work, work your body;

Work your body light.

Work, work, work your body;

Work your body right.

(Chorus)

STOMP AND SHOUT FOLK SONGS

African American children made the following songs a part of their circle games, clapping their hands and stomping their feet in the same way their ancestors had done before them.

DEM BONES

This song was inspired by Ezekiel 37:1–4, where the prophet visits the Valley of the Dry Bones and says they will one day arise at God's command. When my friends and I sang it, we imagined the dry bones reconnecting and tried to imitate how the skeletons might have moved, or we touched the part of our body that was attaching to the rest.

Chorus:

Dem bones, dem bones, dem dry bones.

Dem bones, dem bones, dem dry bones.

Dem bones, dem bones, dem dry bones.

Oh, hear de word of de Lord.

God called Ezekiel by His word:

Say, "Go down and prophesy!"

Ezekiel prophesied by the power of God.

Commanded dem bones to rise.

Then de toe bone connected wid the foot bone.

De foot bone connected wid the ankle bone.

De ankle bone connected wid the leg bone.

46

De leg bone connected wid the thigh bone.

Now hear de word of de Lord!

(Chorus)

Then de thigh bone connected wid the hip bone.

De hip bone connected wid the backbone.

De backbone connected wid the shoulder bone.

De shoulder bone connected wid the neck bone,

And the neck bone holds up the head.

(Chorus)

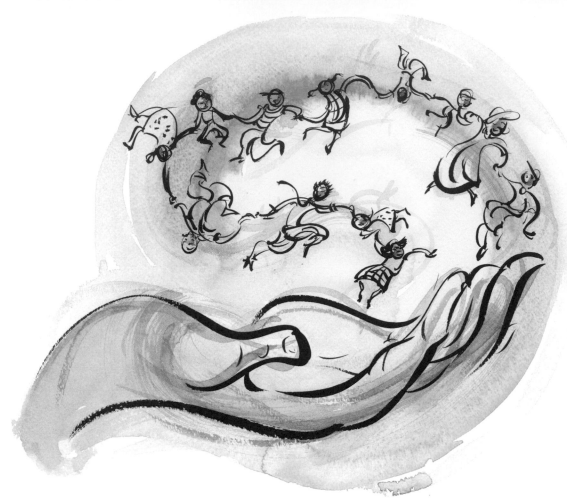

HE'S GOT THE WHOLE WORLD IN HIS HANDS

This song first appeared in print in a 1927 African American hymnal titled Spirituals Triumphant: Old and New. *We always held hands and swayed from side to side when we sang it, as many people still do today.*

He's got the whole world in his hands.

He's got the whole world in his hands.

He's got the big, round world in his hands.

He's got the whole world in his hands.

He's got the wind and rain in his hands.

He's got the wind and rain in his hands.

He's got the wind and rain in his hands.

He's got the whole world in his hands.

He's got the little bitsy baby in his hands.

He's got the little bitsy baby in his hands.

He's got the little bitsy baby in his hands.

He's got the whole world in his hands.

He's got you and me, sister, in his hands.

He's got you and me, sister, in his hands.

He's got you and me, sister, in his hands.

He's got the whole world in his hands.

He's got you and me, brother, in his hands.

He's got you and me, brother, in his hands.

He's got you and me, brother, in his hands.

He's got the whole world in his hands.

KUM BAH YAH

Also known as "Come by Here," "Kumbaya," and "Come by Heah," this is an African American spiritual that was first collected and recorded in the 1920s, as it was sung by the Gullah people. I learned the song while attending Camp Derricotte in Troy, Missouri, when I was ten.

Kum bah yah, my Lord, kum bah yah.

Kum bah yah, my Lord, kum bah yah.

Kum bah yah, my Lord, kum bah yah.

Oh, Lord, kum bah yah.

Someone's crying, my Lord, kum bah yah.

Someone's crying, my Lord, kum bah yah.

Someone's crying, my Lord, kum bah yah.

Oh, Lord, kum bah yah.

Someone's singing, my Lord, kum bah yah.

Someone's singing, my Lord, kum bah yah.

Someone's singing, my Lord, kum bah yah.

Oh, Lord, kum bah yah.

Someone's praying, my Lord, kum bah yah.

Someone's praying, my Lord, kum bah yah.

Someone's praying, my Lord, kum bah yah.

Oh, Lord, kum bah yah.

Chapter 4
FOLLOW THE DRINKING GOURD
SONGS INSPIRED BY THE UNDERGROUND RAILROAD

African slaves communicated their ideas and emotions with music during their long quest for freedom. Many of the songs they created, such as "Steal Away" and "This Train," reflected the experiences of runaways on the Underground Railroad, which was neither under the ground nor a railroad. It was a series of routes along which slaves found their way from bondage in the South to freedom in Canada or in Mexico. On the perilous journey, there were people who helped, called conductors, and stops, known as stations—safe houses where runaways were fed and sheltered until it was time to move on.

Since slaves weren't allowed to hold meetings unless they were monitored by an overseer, they learned how to communicate through coded language, called double speech or double talk. In this way Bible stories and religious music served two purposes. In addition to building faith, the stories and songs were used to secretly convey escape plans and other information, without the slave masters' understanding a word.

My classmates and I were encouraged by our teachers and parents to incorporate this part of our history in play. So we learned the songs and imagined what it must have been like for the runaways. We even put new twists on simple games like hide 'n' seek and catch.

To understand the slaves' coded songs, you first need to understand the double meaning of some of the words. Here is a list:

CODED WORD	SPIRITUAL MEANING	RUNAWAY'S MEANING
Glory	Heaven	Freedom
Home	Heaven	Freedom
Steal away	Die peacefully	Run away
Crossing over	Dying	Crossing into freedom
I aine got long	I'm waiting to die	I'm waiting for a signal to run
This train	A Heaven-bound train	A group of runaways
Jordan	A biblical river	Any river leading to freedom
Chariot	A heavenly vehicle	A conductor who will carry slaves to freedom

THIS GLORY TRAIN

This train is bound for glory, this train.

This train is bound for glory, this train.

This train is bound for glory.

Get on board and tell your story.

This train is bound for glory, this train.

This train don't pull no extras, this train.

This train don't pull no extras, this train.

This train don't pull no extras.

Don't pull nothing but the midnight special.

This train don't pull no extras, this train.

WHEN I GET TO HEAVEN

I've got a robe; you've got a robe.

All God's children got a robe.

When I get to Heav'n goin' to put on my robe,

Goin' to shout all over God's Heav'n.

Heav'n, Heav'n,

Ev'rybody talkin' 'bout Heav'n aine goin' there.

Heav'n, Heav'n,

Goin' to shout all over God's Heav'n.

I've got-a wings, you've got-a wings.

All God's children got-a wings.

When I get to Heav'n goin' to put on my wings,

Goin' to fly all over God's Heav'n.

Heav'n, Heav'n,

Ev'rybody talkin' 'bout Heav'n aine goin' there.

Heav'n, Heav'n,

Goin' to fly all over God's Heav'n.

I've got a harp; you've got a harp.

All God's children got a harp.

When I get to Heav'n goin' to play on my harp,

Make music all over God's Heav'n.

Heav'n, Heav'n,

Ev'rybody talkin' 'bout Heav'n aine goin' there.

Heav'n, Heav'n,

Make music all over God's Heav'n.

GET ON BOARD

Chorus:

Get on board, li'l children;

Get on board, li'l children;

Get on board, li'l children;

There's room for many a-more.

The gospel train is coming;

I hear it just at hand.

I hear the car wheels moving,

And rumbling thro' the land.

(Chorus)

The fare is cheap and all can go;

The rich and poor are there.

No second class aboard this train,

No difference in the fare.

STEAL AWAY

It is believed that a Native American named Wallis Willis might have heard this song while serving as a conductor on the Underground Railroad before the Choctaw were forced to leave the Southern and Southeastern states and relocate to Oklahoma in the 1830s. It was written down by someone who overheard Willis, who then passed it along to the Jubilee Singers (see page 67), who included it in their collection of abolitionist songs.

Chorus:

Steal away, steal away, steal away to Jesus!

Steal away, steal away home.

I aine got long to stay here.

My Lord, He calls me,

He calls me by the thunder.

The trumpet sounds within-a my soul.

I aine got long to stay here.

(Chorus)

Green trees a-bending,

Poor sinner stands a-trembling.

The trumpet sounds within-a my soul.

I aine got long to stay here.

(Chorus)

FOLLOW THE DRINKING GOURD

Peg-Leg Joe, a seaman and a conductor, secretly taught runaways this song, which would lead them through the woods to the Tombigbee River in Alabama, through the hills called the Tennessee Valley Divide, and across the Ohio River to freedom. It was a long and difficult journey, but there was help along the way. Peg-Leg Joe usually went ahead of the runaways and marked the trail by leaving his distinctive prints, which included a hole made by his peg leg.

The North Star, found in the handle of the Little Dipper (the drinking gourd of the song), always indicates north. If runaways got lost, they could follow the North Star until it eventually led them to a safe house or to freedom. My friends and I would gaze at the North Star on a clear evening and imagine what it must have looked like to a runaway long ago.

Chorus:

Follow the drinking gourd.

Follow the drinking gourd.

For the old man's a-waiting for to carry you to freedom.

Follow the drinking gourd.

When the sun comes back and the first quail calls,

Follow the drinking gourd.

For the old man's a-waiting for to carry you to freedom.

Follow the drinking gourd.

(Chorus)

Now, the riverbank will make a mighty good road.

The dead trees will show you the way.

Left foot, peg foot, traveling on,

Just follow the drinking gourd.

(Chorus)

Now, the river ends between two hills.

Follow the drinking gourd.

And there's another river on the other side.

Follow the drinking gourd.

(Chorus)

Where the great big river meets the little river,

Follow the drinking gourd.

The old man's a-waiting for to carry you to freedom.

Follow the drinking gourd.

SWING LOW, SWEET CHARIOT

Harriet Tubman's childhood nickname was Minty, but Moses became her name among slaves. Born a slave, she escaped to Philadelphia when she was in her twenties. There she was helped by Quaker abolitionists, eventually becoming one of the Underground Railroad's most famous conductors. After first leading her family to freedom, she returned to the South on nineteen different missions and never lost a passenger. Tubman led more than three hundred slaves to freedom, often using her favorite song: "Swing Low, Sweet Chariot."

Chorus:

Swing low, sweet chariot,

Comin' for to carry me home.

Swing low, sweet chariot,

Comin' for to carry me home.

I looked over Jordan,

And what did I see,

Comin' for to carry me home?

A band of angels comin' after me,

Comin' for to carry me home.

(Chorus)

If you get there before I do,

Comin' for to carry me home,

Tell all my friends I'm a-comin', too,

Comin' for to carry me home.

(Chorus)

Chapter 5
MAKE A JOYFUL NOISE
SPIRITUALS, HYMNS, AND GOSPEL MUSIC

Spirituals, hymns, and gospel music were the songs that slaves sang in worship, in obedience to Psalm 98:4 in the King James Version of the Bible: "Make a joyful noise unto the Lord, all the earth: make a loud noise, and rejoice and sing praise." Today, the rich sounds of old slave songs still ring out in religious institutions of many denominations throughout the world. I learned most of the songs that follow at an early age and sang them in my church and school choirs.

After the Civil War, choirs and small groups were organized by those who wanted to preserve the music of the former slaves, and to teach their children the important contribution our people made to New World music.

As early as age six, I sang in the church choir with all of my grade school friends. One of the most memorable parts of making "a joyful noise" was hearing the history behind these marvelous songs. Later in life, my children asked me to share these songs and stories with them. I did, and now I will share them with you.

SPIRITUALS

Spirituals originated in the fields and slave quarters of the plantation South. They passed from one generation to another, but after slavery ended, very few had been written down or scored. Many of them would have been lost if not for the Jubilee Singers of Fisk University.

Fisk University, one of America's oldest and most prestigious colleges, came into being in 1867, in Nashville, to educate former slaves from ages five to seventy-five. In 1871, the school formed a musical group called the Jubilee Singers, who collected and preserved the songs of their parents and grandparents—songs that otherwise might have been lost forever. They toured the country and earned rave reviews for their concerts. Two classic spirituals among the Fisk collection are "Joshua Fit the Battle of Jericho" and "Sometimes I Feel Like a Motherless Child."

JOSHUA FIT (FOUGHT) THE BATTLE OF JERICHO

Chorus:

Joshua fit the battle of Jericho,

Jericho, Jericho.

Joshua fit the Battle of Jericho,

And the walls came tumblin' down.

You may talk about your king of Gideon.

You may talk about your men of Saul.

But none like good ol' Joshua

At the Battle of Jericho.

(Chorus)

(Chorus)

Up to the walls of Jericho,

He marched with spear in hand.

"Go blow them ram horns," Joshua cried.

"'Cause the battle is in my hands."

(Chorus)

Then the lamb ram sheep horns began to blow.

The trumpets began to sound.

Joshua commanded the children to shout,

And the walls came tumblin' down.

(Chorus)

Down, down, down, down,

And the walls came tumblin' down.

SOMETIMES I FEEL LIKE A MOTHERLESS CHILD

Sometimes I feel like a motherless child,

Sometimes I feel like a motherless child,

Sometimes I feel like a motherless child,

A long ways from home.

A long ways from home.

Sometimes I feel like I'm almos' gone,

Sometimes I feel like I'm almos' gone,

Sometimes I feel like I'm almos' gone,

A long ways from home.

A long ways from home.

OH, FREEDOM

Under the strong leadership of Dr. Martin Luther King, Jr., and others, the modern civil rights movement pushed for freedom and justice for all Americans. During their demonstrations throughout the 1960s and 1970s, civil rights leaders adopted old spirituals and gospel songs as they marched in protest. Probably the most famous was "We Shall Overcome," but there were many others, including "We Shall Not Be Moved," "Walk Together, Children, Don't You Get Weary," and my favorite, "Oh, Freedom." During the movement, the lyrics of this historical music took on new meaning and gave those who sang the protest songs a sense of determination and commitment not felt since the days of the abolitionists.

Although I was too young to be involved in the marches, my friends and I did what we could. We attended meetings, stuffed envelopes, and ran errands. We also cheered for new heroes in our circle shouts and dances and jumped for joy when an unjust law was struck down by the courts. And of course, we sang the songs.

Today, the civil rights movement and the protest songs associated with it are inseparable. People all over the globe who seek equal rights, freedom, and justice very often sing these powerful songs.

Oh, freedom, oh, freedom, oh, freedom over me!

And before I'd be a slave, I'll be buried in my grave

And go home to my Lord and be free.

No more moaning, no more moaning,
  no more moaning over me!
And before I'd be a slave, I'll be buried
  in my grave
And go home to my Lord and be free.

No more weeping, no more weeping, no more weeping over me!
And before I'd be a slave, I'll be buried in my grave
And go home to my Lord and be free.

There'll be singin', there'll be singin', there'll be singin' over me!
And before I'd be a slave, I'll be buried in my grave
And go home to my Lord and be free.

There'll be shoutin', there'll be shoutin', there'll be shoutin' over me!
And before I'd be a slave, I'll be buried in my grave
And go home to my Lord and be free.

There'll be prayin', there'll be prayin', there'll be prayin' over me!
And before I'd be a slave, I'll be buried in my grave
And go home to my Lord and be free.

Oh, freedom, oh, freedom, oh, freedom over me!
And before I'd be a slave, I'll be buried in my grave
And go home to my Lord and be free.

HYMNS

A hymn is a religious poem or song meant to be spoken or sung by worshippers in praise of God and God's purpose in human life. The earliest hymns date back to ancient China, Egypt, and Greece.

Today there are hundreds of hymns that are loved and sung regularly by people all over the world. I learned hymns from my mother during nighttime prayers, at Sunday school, and even from my friends at play. Here are several examples of hymns still popular among African American children.

JESUS LOVES ME

Jesus loves me, this I know,

For the Bible tells me so.

Little ones to Him belong,

They are weak, but He is strong.

Chorus:

Yes, Jesus loves me.

Yes, Jesus loves me.

Yes, Jesus loves me,

The Bible tells me so.

Jesus loves me! He will stay

Close beside me all the way.

Thou hast bled and died for me,

I will hence-forth live for thee.

(Chorus)

JESUS LOVES THE LITTLE CHILDREN

Jesus calls the children dear,

"Come to me and never fear,

For I love the little children of the world,

I will take you by the hand,

Lead you to the better land,

For I love the little children of the world."

Chorus:

Jesus loves the little children,

All the children of the world.

Red and yellow, black and white,

All are precious in His sight.

Jesus loves the little children of the world.

Jesus is the Shepherd true,

And He'll always stand by you,

For He loves the little children of the world;

He's a Savior great and strong,

And He'll shield you from the wrong,

For He loves the little children of the world.

(Chorus)

I am coming, Lord, to Thee,

And Your soldier I will be,

For You love the little children of the world;

And Your cross I'll always bear,

And for You I'll do and dare,

For You love the little children of the world.

I'LL BE A SUNBEAM

Jesus wants me for a sunbeam,

To shine for Him each day;

In every way try to please Him,

At home, at school, at play.

Chorus:

A sunbeam, a sunbeam,

Jesus wants me for a sunbeam;

A sunbeam, a sunbeam,

I'll be a sunbeam for Him.

Jesus wants me to be loving,

And kind to all I see;

Showing how pleasant and happy

His little one can be.

(Chorus)

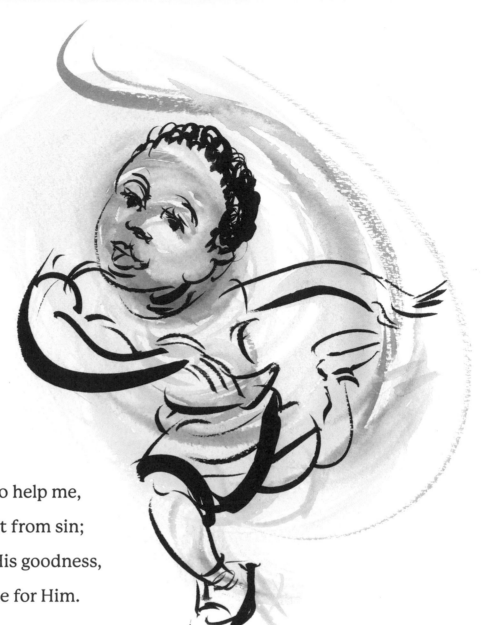

I will ask Jesus to help me,
To keep my heart from sin;
Ever reflecting His goodness,
And always shine for Him.

(Chorus)

I'll be a sunbeam for Jesus,
I can if I but try;
Serving Him moment by moment,
Then live for Him on high.

(Chorus)

GOSPEL MUSIC

Gospel music, which dates back to the 1700s, is more about the way the songs are delivered than about the lyrics. Gospel is performed with lively emotions and includes clapping, swaying, hand waving, and shouts of joy. It usually praises the life of Jesus as it is recounted in the first four books of the New Testament—the Gospels—Matthew, Mark, Luke, and John. During slavery times, spirituals were sung in gospel style. During the 1920s, composers began writing original gospel songs, and these became a separate category of worship music.

THIS LITTLE LIGHT OF MINE

My sixth-grade choir, directed by Mrs. Johnetta Haley, performed this using flashlights with tissue covering the top to imitate a flame. We held these makeshift candles while singing.

This little light of mine,

I'm going to let it shine.

This little light of mine,

I'm going to let it shine.

This little light of mine,

Hallelujah,

I'm going to let it shine.

Let it shine, let it shine, let it shine.

All in my house *(call)*,

I'm going to let it shine. *(response)*

All in my house *(call)*,

I'm going to let it shine. *(response)*

All in my house, Hallelujah, *(call)*

I'm going to let it shine. *(response)*

Let it shine, let it shine, let it shine. *(together)*

Everywhere I go *(as before)*,

I'm going to let it shine.

Everywhere I go,

I'm going to let it shine.

Everywhere I go,

Hallelujah,

I'm going to let it shine.

Let it shine, let it shine, let it shine.

(Add more verses using call-and-response.)

GIVE ME THAT OLD-TIME RELIGION

This traditional gospel song dates back to 1873, when it was included in a list of songs preserved by the Fisk Jubilee Singers collection.

Give me that old-time religion.

Give me that old-time religion.

Give me that old-time religion.

It's good enough for me.

It was good for Paul and Silas.

It was good for Paul and Silas.

It was good for Paul and Silas.

It's good enough for me.

It was good for the children of Abraham.

It was good for the children of Abraham.

It was good for the children of Abraham.

It's good enough for me.

It was good for the prophet Daniel.

It was good for the prophet Daniel.

It was good for the prophet Daniel.

It's good enough for me.

(Add another name for each new verse.)

PRECIOUS LORD, TAKE MY HAND

In 1932, a grief-stricken musician and composer named Thomas Dorsey, whose wife had just died during childbirth and whose newborn baby had died two days later, wrote "Precious Lord, Take My Hand." It has become a gospel classic.

The civil rights leader Dr. Martin Luther King, Jr., liked the song very much. Knowing this, the choir sang "Precious Lord" at the 1968 rally led by Dr. King in Memphis; little did they know that this was the night before his assassination. A few days later, Mahalia Jackson sang it at Dr. King's funeral. It was also a favorite of President Lyndon B. Johnson, who requested that it be sung at his own funeral. It was sung at my grandmother's funeral as well.

Precious Lord, take my hand,

Lead me on, let me stand.

I am tired; I am weak; I'm worn.

Through the storm, through the night,

Lead me on to the light.

Take my hand, Precious Lord,

Lead me home.

When my way grows drear,

Precious Lord, linger near.

When my life is almost gone,

Hear my cry, hear my call,

Hold my hand, lest I fall.

Take my hand, Precious Lord,

Lead me home.

When the darkness appears

And the night draws near,

And the day is past and gone,

At the river I stand,

Guide my feet, hold my hand.

Take my hand, precious Lord.

Lead me home.

I'LL FLY AWAY

When I was in grade school I first heard the story of Ibo Landing, on St. Simons Island, Georgia. Later, I visited the island, and I was overwhelmed as the story was told by the Georgia Sea Island Singers, Doug and Frankie Quimby, at the site of the event along Dunbar Creek.

According to the story, in 1803 eighteen Ibo African captives decided they would rather die than be enslaved. The Ibo (also known as Igbo) people were from southeastern Nigeria. They linked themselves together, arm in arm, walked into the water, and drowned.

The other Africans who witnessed the drowning reported seeing a flock of beautiful birds, never before spotted in that part of the world, rise up immediately after and fly eastward out to sea, toward Africa. And so for them, it wasn't a sad story. From that time on, storytellers have projected the happening as a wonderful example of hope and determination.

When I tell this story I always couple it with the song "I'll Fly Away," written by Albert E. Brumley.

Some glad morning when this life is o'er

I'll fly away;

To a home on God's celestial shore,

I'll fly away (I'll fly away).

Chorus:

I'll fly away, Oh Glory,

I'll fly away (in the morning);

When I die, Hallelujah, by and by,

I'll fly away (I'll fly away).

When the shadows of this life have gone,

I'll fly away;

Like a bird from prison bars has flown,

I'll fly away (I'll fly away).

(Chorus)

Just a few more weary days and then

I'll fly away;

To a land where joy shall never end,

I'll fly away (I'll fly away).

(Chorus)

AMAZING GRACE

"Amazing Grace" is probably the most beloved gospel song in the world. But what is truly amazing is the story behind the song. It was written by an Englishman named John Newton, a crew member of the Greyhound, *a slave ship. Imagine a black choir singing a song written by a slave runner!*

According to the report by the Greyhound's *captain, Newton was the most vulgar person his captain had ever known; he cursed constantly and even made up words to push the limits of his profanity.*

In March 1748, the Greyhound *was caught in a storm in the North Atlantic. Men were swept overboard, but Newton tied himself to the ship's pump to save himself. He hadn't prayed in years and he wasn't sure God would hear him, but he prayed anyway. The storm passed and the ship was saved. About two weeks later, the* Greyhound *limped into Lough Swilly, Ireland.*

Thereafter, Newton was never quite the same.

His conversion was not immediate, as some historians suggest. He continued to serve on slave ships for several more years and was even elevated to the rank of captain of his own. Still, he continued to seek answers and to ponder what he thought was right and wrong. After he stopped slaving, he joined a church and studied the Gospels. In 1750 he had married a devout Christian woman named Mary (Polly) Catlett, and they became hardworking church members.

Newton began studying Greek and Latin. After years of struggle, he accepted his call to become a minister. He wrote about his experiences in the slave trade and his conversion. The Earl of Dartmouth sponsored him for ordination in the Church of England by the Bishop of Lincoln. Reverend Newton was then assigned to a church in Olney, Buckinghamshire, in 1764. It was there that he wrote "Amazing Grace," a song about redemption.

Amazing grace, how sweet the sound,

That sav'd a wretch like me!

I once was lost, but now am found,

Was blind, but now I see.

'Twas grace that taught my heart to fear,

And grace my fears reliev'd;

How precious did that grace appear

The hour I first believ'd!

Through many dangers, toils, and snares,

I have already come;

'Tis grace hath brought me safe thus far,

And grace will lead me home.

The Lord has promis'd good to me,

His word my hope secures;

He will my shield and portion be

As long as life endures.

Yes, when this flesh and heart shall fail,

And mortal life shall cease;

I shall possess, within the veil,

A life of joy and peace.

The earth shall soon dissolve like snow,

The sun forbear to shine;

But God, who call'd me here below,

Will be forever mine.

Chapter 6
PEARLS OF WISDOM
PROVERBS, PSALMS, AND PARABLES

And now abideth faith, hope, and charity, these three, but the greatest of these is charity.

1 Corinthians 13:13, King James Version

Faith, hope, and charity (love for others) were the pearls of wisdom upon which my childhood moral code was based. Proverbs, psalms, and parables were the tools used to teach these important principles.

African American churches lent strong support to the civil rights movement and its goals, and our Sunday school teachers (who were sometimes our teachers in public school) infused our lessons with parallels between the subjugation of our ancestors and our own segregated society. I remember participating in exercises to see who could memorize the most psalms or proverbs that were good examples of faith and hope. We also told parables from other cultures that illustrated how we could practice peace and respect for others.

And never were these pearls of wisdom needed more than in the struggle to sustain the nonviolent revolution led by Dr. Martin Luther King, Jr. Dr. King found messages of faith, hope, and love among all religions and united them for a common cause—peace and freedom. It was an exciting time, and I loved being involved.

PROVERBS

A proverb is a saying that states a truth, and helps instruct those who seek wisdom, judgment, and equity. The proverbs that have influenced African American society are found in the holy books of the major religions—the Christian Bible, the Jewish Torah, and the Muslim Qur'an. Others come from Chinese Confucianism, Hinduism, and Native American cultures. Interestingly, many of the proverbs are similar from culture to culture. For example, some version of "You can't buy love" can be found in countries all over the world.

One of the best known proverbs that has influenced many African Americans is Proverbs 6:16–19, which states "These six things doth the Lord hate: yea, seven are an abomination unto him: a proud look, a lying tongue, and hands that shed innocent blood, an heart that deviseth wicked imaginations, feet that be swift in running to mischief, a false witness that speaketh lies, and he that soweth discord among brethren." Many cultures have wise sayings with many of the themes found in this passage. These are a few.

AFRICAN SAYING

Even though you may be taller, stronger,

and younger than your father, you are still not his equal.

AFRICAN AMERICAN SAYING

Respect your elders.

*

AFRICAN SAYING

Only those of the same nature gather together—

thief to thief, liar to liar.

AFRICAN AMERICAN SAYING

A thief knows a thief, and a liar knows a liar.

So remember, birds of a feather flock together.

AFRICAN SAYING
"I will do it later" is the brother of "I didn't get around to doing it."

AFRICAN AMERICAN SAYING
Too often "I mean to do it" becomes "I meant to do it."

*

MUSLIM SAYING
Control your tongue.

AFRICAN AMERICAN SAYING
Make sure your tongue isn't like a tiger whose tail is on fire—
angry and painful.

NATIVE AMERICAN SAYING

The canoe must be paddled on both sides.

AFRICAN AMERICAN SAYING

We must work together or starve separately.

*

CONFUCIAN SAYING

Forget injuries; never forget a kindness.

AFRICAN AMERICAN SAYING

Do whatever you do for others willingly,
and always with a smiling heart.

*

NATIVE AMERICAN SAYING

Do not allow anger to poison you.

AFRICAN AMERICAN SAYING

There is no medicine that can cure hatred or cruelty.

NATIVE AMERICAN SAYING

Be satisfied with the needs instead of the wants.

AFRICAN AMERICAN SAYING

There's nothing better than enough.

✳

JEWISH SAYING

The confidence of fools will destroy them.

AFRICAN AMERICAN SAYING

Never be ashamed of asking. The shame is in boasting
about what you know, when you don't know a thing.

✳

BIBLICAL PROVERB—PROVERBS 1:10

My son, if sinners entice thee, consent thou not.

AFRICAN AMERICAN SAYING

Shun evil.

✳

BIBLICAL PROVERB—MATTHEW 7:12

Therefore all things whatsoever ye would that men should do to you,
do ye even so to them: for this is the law and the prophets.

AFRICAN AMERICAN SAYING

Treat others the way you want to be treated.

PSALMS

A psalm is a sacred poem of praise. Sometimes it is sung, accompanied by a harp or flute.

THE FIRST PSALM

David was a shepherd boy who watched over his father's sheep. At night when wild animals threatened the small lambs, David would play his harp and sing prayers of comfort, joy, love, mercy, forgiveness, and faith. The opening verses of the Book of Psalms make up one of David's best-loved songs.

Blessed is the man that walketh not in the counsel of the

ungodly, nor standeth in the way of sinners, nor sitteth

in the seat of the scornful.

But his delight is in the law of the Lord; and in his law doth

    he meditate day and night.

And he shall be like a tree planted by the rivers of water,

    that bringeth forth his fruit in his season; his leaf also

    shall not wither; and whatsoever he doeth

    shall prosper.

THE TWENTY-THIRD PSALM

The Bible tells us that before David became King of the Hebrews, he made a name for himself by using a slingshot and five smooth stones to slay the Philistine giant Goliath, who was devastating the Hebrew army. The psalms of David remind us of God's promise to be a good shepherd to all. The Twenty-Third Psalm expresses that promise eloquently, and it is usually the first that African American children commit to memory.

The Lord is my shepherd; I shall not want.

He maketh me to lie down in green pastures: he leadeth

    me beside the still waters.

He restoreth my soul: he leadeth me in the paths of

    righteousness for his name's sake.

Yea, though I walk through the valley of the shadow of

    death, I will fear no evil: for thou art with me; thy rod

    and thy staff they comfort me.

Thou preparest a table before me in the presence of mine enemies:

thou anointest my head with oil; my cup runneth over.

Surely goodness and mercy shall follow me all the days of my life:

and I will dwell in the house of the Lord forever.

PARABLES

Parables are short stories that teach a moral or spiritual lesson by using analogies or comparisons. The parables I knew were the parables of Jesus found in the New Testament. As a child, I believed that such stories were invented and told only by Jesus. Of course, I was wrong. Parables have been used as teaching tools in many cultures for centuries, beginning before Jesus was born.

My ancestors arrived in the New World with knowledge of the parables, which had been shared with them by Jewish and Muslim traders. When these spiritual stories were introduced to them again by their European captors, the slaves embraced them.

The biblical parables of Jesus are the foundation of many African Americans' spiritual lives. Let me share a few of my favorites.

THE PRODIGAL SON

Retold from Luke 15:11–32, King James Version

"Prodigal" means wasteful, reckless, or extravagant. The lesson is how important each one of us is to God.

A man had two sons. One day the younger son went to his father and said, "Father, give me my inheritance now, because I want to leave this place." His father gave each son his share of his estate, and the younger son left.

He went to town and fell in with a bad crowd. He gambled, drank heavily, and spent money wildly, until a famine came to the land. Now the son had nothing. Broke and alone, he worked in a pigpen and coveted the slop the swine ate. Then he thought, *I made a mistake, but I don't have to live like this. I will go home to my father's house, where even his servants eat well.*

So the younger son headed back home. When his father saw him, he ran out to greet the boy. They hugged each other and rejoiced. "My son, my son, you have come back to me!" the man cried.

"I was wrong, Father," said the son. "I have come to beg your forgiveness."

The father called for his servants to bring a clean robe for his son, and a ring for his finger, and to kill a calf and prepare a feast. "We will rejoice and be happy that my child has returned to us," the father commanded.

The older son, who had always been faithful and had done everything he could to be helpful, was upset. "Father, I have been loyal, but you've never

95

had a party for me. Here my brother goes off and lives a notorious life and you welcome him home with a great celebration. I don't understand it."

The father embraced his older son. "I love you and I always will. Everything I have is yours. But your brother was separated from us, and he has come home. He was lost, but now he has been found. Let us rejoice and be glad."

THE GOOD SAMARITAN

Retold from Luke 10:25–37, King James Version

Samaritans—ancient Hebrews from Samaria—were considered people of poor character and were shunned for their lifestyle. This parable illustrates how we should not judge each other, but should treat people with respect and kindness.

A Hebrew man was traveling down the road when some thieves attacked him, stole his money and all his goods, beat him, and left him to die. The Hebrew cried out for help as a priest came by. The priest looked at the injured man, but he was in a hurry, so he convinced himself the man wasn't that badly off and left him there for someone else to help.

Soon a Levite—a member of the Hebrew tribe of Levi—came by. The injured man recognized him as a merchant from a neighboring village, but the Levite crossed the street to avoid getting involved.

Finally a Samaritan came by on his donkey and, seeing the Hebrew beside the road, stopped to help. The Samaritan lifted the injured man onto his donkey and gave him water. Then the Samaritan took the man to the nearest town and paid for his food and a place to stay until he was able to travel. The Samaritan promised to stop by on his way home to see how the injured man was healing and to take care of any additional expenses.

The Hebrew was genuinely surprised, but he was also very grateful, for the Good Samaritan had gone beyond what was expected of a stranger.

THE MUSTARD SEED

Retold from Matthew 13:31–32, King James Version
This parable uses the mustard seed as a metaphor for faith.

The mustard seed is the smallest of all seeds. When planted, it grows, and grows, and grows—slowly. In good time, and with good care, it soars into a huge tree where the birds of the air come and perch. Such is the Kingdom of Heaven. So is your faith. It grows and grows and grows, and in time and with care, it becomes filled with the spiritual fruits of goodness and mercy.

Chapter 7
A WORD TO THE WISE
SUPERSTITIONS, FABLES, AND MAMA SAYINGS

Superstitions and fables serve as warnings to keep children free from harm, to build moral character, and to help us all live together in harmony. These folk beliefs are as old as human communication, and no single culture can be credited with creating them. Most superstitions and fables have been passed from generation to generation by elders of the community and repeated by children in their play.

Mama sayings or apron wisdom are examples of folk wisdom that has been passed by African American women to their children and grandchildren forever. Like most African American mothers, my mama always put her own twists on the wisdom and made sure we understood what she was telling us—so that we kids could never say we didn't know any better!

SUPERSTITIONS

People are superstitious. Some may not play a game or take a trip unless they wear a lucky pair of socks; others will eat black-eyed peas on New Year's Day, believing that this practice will bring them money all year. Although superstitions are not taken as seriously as they were several centuries ago, folks still wear good-luck charms and amulets for fun—or maybe just in case. . . .

Many superstitions that are part of African American culture can be traced to West Africa, the Caribbean Islands, and especially New Orleans, where some people still believe in spells.

African American children have embraced the superstitions of other immigrants, too, such as the Irish, Hungarians, Romanians, and Bulgarians. Their folklore includes stories about genies, leprechauns, witches, vampires, and werewolves—the source of some very scary beliefs. Even today, I still wear a small gold cross to ward off a vampire attack.

GOOD LUCK AND HAPPY SUPERSTITIONS

A horseshoe hung over a doorway will keep evil spirits away.

*

A cricket in your house is good luck.
(Don't kill it, because that's bad luck.)

*

Seven is a lucky number, especially for gamblers.

*

A rabbit's foot is a good-luck charm.

*

Eating fresh fish makes you smart.

If you blow out all the candles on your birthday cake in one breath, you'll get your wish.

*

If you drop a spoon, a hungry child is coming.

*

If you drop a fork, a pregnant woman is coming.

*

Put stone lions or dragons on your porch or in your garden to keep away evil spirits and witches.

*

Cold hands, warm heart.

BAD LUCK AND UNHAPPY SUPERSTITIONS

Get out of bed on the same side you got in,
otherwise you'll have bad luck all day.

✳

Thirteen is an unlucky number.

✳

Six hundred sixty-six is the unlucky number of the devil.

✳

Don't put new shoes on a bed. They will never fit well.

✳

Spilling salt is bad luck, unless you gather a few grains and throw
them over your left shoulder to break the spell.

✳

If you drop a knife, an uninvited guest will
show up just in time for dinner.

When a wild bird gets into the house, it is an omen of death.

✳

A groom should never see his bride on their wedding day,
for it is bad luck.

✳

Beware of a strange cat around an infant.
The cat might be a witch's agent.

PORCH SCHOOL

Here is a game that was popular from the 1950s through the 1970s. Players found front or back steps that had six or more risers and selected a "teacher," who then determined what the subject would be—Bible stories, baseball, movies, or whatever.

The players sat on the bottom step, which represented first grade. The "teacher" asked questions and the "students" answered. Pupils were "promoted" to the next step with each correct answer. If students answered incorrectly, they were "left behind," staying in the same grade (on the same step) until they answered correctly. Those who reached the top step graduated.

Here are a set of porch school questions like the ones we used. They are based on superstitions we all knew and recognized.

Question: What happens if you sweep a young girl's feet?

Answer: She'll never get married.

Question: Name two things that are bad luck.

Answer: Hanging a purse on a doorknob and looking in a mirror at midnight on Friday the thirteenth and saying,
"Come, Hannah McBride."

Question: When your eye twitches, what's going to happen?

Answer: You'll see someone you haven't seen in a long time.

Question: Name two things that are considered good luck.

Answer: Finding a four-leaf clover and finding a penny heads up.

Question: Garlic is good for . . . ?
Answer: Keeping vampires away.

Question: If you hear a hoot owl at night, what is that a sign of?
Answer: Death.

Question: What color is the cat that causes you bad luck if it crosses your path—left to right?
Answer: Black.

Question: If you break a mirror, it will bring you . . . ?
Answer: Seven years of bad luck.

Question: To ensure good luck all year, on New Year's Day, you must eat what?
Answer: Black-eyed peas and greens.

Question: It's impolite and also bad luck to talk when your . . .
Answer: Mouth is full of food.

Question: Is it good luck or bad luck to open an umbrella
 in the house?
Answer: Bad luck.

FABLES

A fable is a short narrative in which talking animals, trees, birds, and other nonhuman characters are used to teach an important life lesson.

The best-known fables were by Aesop. There is an ongoing debate among scholars about who he really was, but it is believed he was an Afro-Greek storyteller who lived as a slave approximately twenty-five hundred years ago. The stories that bear his name continue to be a part of many African Americans' childhood.

To know that Aesop was a man of color from long ago gives young black children someone to honor. Aesop's Fables are shared at family storytelling sessions and when parents want to teach their children a lesson without being preachy. Aesop concluded each story with a statement about the lesson being taught.

THE ANT AND THE DOVE

A tiny ant came to a stream. He needed to get to the other side, so he jumped in and started to swim across. But the current was too strong and he was swept away, sure to drown.

Meanwhile, a dove that was sitting on a tree branch saw the little ant struggling, so she plucked a leaf from the tree and dropped it in front of the tiny ant, who climbed on and was saved.

Sometime later, the ant saw a hunter setting a trap for the unsuspecting dove. The ant hurried to the spot and bit the trapper on his foot, which made him scream. The dove heard the noise and flew away to safety.

One good deed deserves another.

THE BEAR AND THE TWO TRAVELERS

Two friends were traveling together when suddenly a bear burst from the bushes and attacked them. One man quickly climbed into a tree and hid. The man on the ground cried out for help—but his friend did nothing. So the man, defenseless, fell to the ground and pretended to be dead. The

bear nudged him and flipped him over, but the traveler kept his eyes shut, held his breath, and remained lifeless. At last, the bear lumbered away. The friend in the tree hurried down, while the one on the ground sat up and let out a sigh of relief. "So glad you are alive, my friend," said the man who had hidden in the tree. "No credit to you," said the friend on the ground.

Trouble puts friendship to a real test.

THE FROGS AND THE BOYS

Several boys came to a pond and saw some frogs sitting on a log. One picked up a stone and threw it at a frog. The injured frog flipped over in pain. The other boys followed suit, hurling rock after rock. The unfortunate frogs were bloody and broken, but the boys had fun.

What is pleasure to one may be misery and pain to another.

THE DOG AND THE WOLF

Dr. Martin Luther King, Jr., included an Aesop story in his speeches. He told "The Dog and the Wolf" in his speech at Fisk University on April 20, 1960, after the bombing of the home of the civil rights attorney Z. Alexander Looby in Nashville. Over four thousand people came to hear Dr. King. I was among them.

A starving wolf slipped out of the woods one night in search of something—anything—to eat. He came upon a stable, where he hoped there might be some chickens, or maybe a goat. Instead he found his cousin, Dog.

"What are you doing here?" Dog asked. "You never come near humans."

"I am hungry, cousin. I have come in search of food," replied Wolf.

Dog responded pleasantly. "Cousin, welcome. Eat with me. My master sees that I have plenty, enough to share. Please partake."

Wolf gratefully accepted the offer and ate well. After a good meal, the cousins discussed the wolf's situation. Wolf explained how hunters had taken so many rabbits, wild turkeys, and muskrats, there wasn't anything left for him and his family to eat. "What did you do to have all this comfort?" Wolf asked Dog.

"I became domesticated. You should try it."

"What does that mean?" Wolf asked.

"I guard my master's property and his house."

"I could do that," responded Wolf.

Dog continued. "I protect his family, especially the children."

"I could do that, too," Wolf said, nodding.

"I watch over his chickens, his donkey, his garden. Everything that is his, is mine to protect."

"I could do that," said Wolf. But then he noticed a chain hanging around a post nearby. "What is that for?" he asked, feeling a bit uneasy.

"Oh, that's my chain," Dog answered matter-of-factly. "Master puts it around my neck each night to make sure I don't run away."

Wolf was shocked. "Chained!" he said, recoiling at the mere mention of it. "You have all this, yet you have no freedom. I thank you for your hospitality, but I must be on my way." And Wolf quickly disappeared into the night.

Some would rather starve than live without freedom.

THE FROGS AND JUPITER

The frogs wanted a new ruler, so they petitioned Jupiter, king of the Roman gods, to help them. So Jupiter sent them a fine leader, but the frogs didn't like him. They begged Jupiter to please reconsider and send them another ruler, which he did. But soon the frogs were back at Jupiter's door, pleading for another. Once again Jupiter did what they asked. But it wasn't long before the frogs were complaining yet again. Each ruler had some flaw that made him or her unsatisfactory. And the last one was no different. Before the year was over, the frogs were calling on Jupiter to replace him. And he did! But this time, Jupiter sent the frogs a crocodile as their ruler. And that was the end of that.

Best to leave well enough alone.

MAMA SAYINGS

Sitting on the front porch with family and neighbors, African American women have often included one-liners in their talk, to have fun, to teach, or to scold. Many of these aphorisms were used by my mother and grandmother. Children who grew up hearing these quips have no doubt used the clever remarks themselves. I know I have!

Every dog's got its day.

✳

Don't wear out welcome.

✳

Kindness is not a weakness.

✳

Everybody uses the bridge they can walk on without a toll.

✳

Fool me once, shame on you; fool me twice, shame on me.

✳

Can't put handsome (pretty) in a pot.

✳

A drowning man will grab a brick.

✳

You can't give a fox the job of watching the chickens.

You kill my dog, I kill your cat. Nobody wins.

＊

A fool and his money will soon part.

＊

Good friends are scarce as hens' teeth.

＊

You never miss your water till the well dries up.

＊

Never do wrong expecting it to turn out right.

＊

It's a poor cook who doesn't get enough to eat.

＊

Remember, the people you step on going up are the same folks
you meet going down!

＊

Best be remembered by what you do, rather than what you said
you were going to do.

＊

Monkey see, monkey do.

＊

Words can't kill your body, but words can kill your spirit.

＊

Evil can't enter your home without being invited to come in.

＊

You must crawl before you walk.

Chapter 8
ON PROGRAM
PERFORMANCE PIECES INSPIRED BY AFRICAN AMERICAN WRITERS

When I was a child, being "on program" meant performing a literary work by an African American writer to celebrate a holiday or festival. The performances were usually sponsored by a church, school, YMCA camp, or social club. I remember working hard to memorize my selections to make sure I didn't make a mistake and embarrass myself and my family.

Many of the pieces my friends and I performed were poems and skits by writers who were part of a period known as the Harlem Renaissance. From 1919 to 1935, an unprecedented number of literary works were produced by black writers. New York City's Harlem was the epicenter of this talent explosion, which rocked the world with fresh ideas in art, music, dance, and literature. However, the most popular poet for an on-program piece was Paul Laurence Dunbar, who was the first postslavery African American to make his living as a full-time writer. Dunbar was not a part of the Harlem Renaissance, but he influenced many writers of that era.

My mother introduced me to Dunbar and the Harlem Renaissance poets when I was very young. We'd sit on the front porch in the wooden swing and she'd read or recite from memory pieces from Dunbar's *Oak and Ivy* and other classics. Other poets who resonated with me—and continue to do so today—are James Weldon Johnson and Langston Hughes.

PAUL LAURENCE DUNBAR (1872–1906)

Paul Laurence Dunbar was born in Dayton, Ohio, in 1872. His parents, Joshua and Matilda, had been slaves, freed after the Civil War. Since Paul was the first of their children to be born free, his parents had a lot of hope for his future. He was a sickly child but was well cared for and managed to have a typically active childhood. He attended school and played games with his friends and neighbors, among them Orville and Wilbur Wright.

My mother used to read Dunbar to me at bedtime, and when she'd finish a piece, I'd beg her to read another and another, until at last she'd send me off to bed.

In addition to writing in standard English, Dunbar wrote using dialect—the language his family used during slavery. Unlike the dialect used in Joel Chandler Harris's Uncle Remus stories, which was viewed by African Americans as stereotypical, Dunbar's dialect was authentic.

LITTLE BROWN BABY

While working as an elevator operator, Dunbar wrote his first collection,
Oak and Ivy, *published in 1893. It included this poem.*

Little brown baby wif spa'klin' eyes,

Come to yo' pappy an' set on his knee.

What you been doin', suh—makin' san' pies?

Look at dat bib—you's ez du'ty ez me.

Look at dat mouf—dat's merlasses, I bet;

Come hyeah, Maria, an' wipe off his han's.

Bees gwine to ketch you an' eat you up yit,

Bein' so sticky an' sweet—goodness lan's!

Little brown baby wif spa'klin' eyes,

Who's pappy's darlin' an' who's pappy's chile?

Who is it all de day nevah once tries

Fu' to be cross, er once loses dat smile?

Whah did you git dem teef? My, you's a scamp!

Whah did dat dimple come f'om in yo' chin?

Pappy do' know you—I b'lieves you's a tramp;

Mammy, dis hyeah's some ol' straggler got in!

Let's th'ow him outen de do' in de san',

We do' want stragglers a-layin' 'roun' hyeah;

Let's gin him 'way to de big buggah-man;

I know he's hidin' erroun' hyeah right neah.

Buggah-man, buggah-man, come in de do',

Hyeah's a bad boy you kin have fu' to eat.

Mammy an' pappy do' want him no mo',

Swaller him down f'om his haid to his feet!

Dah, now, I t'ought dat you'd hug me up close.

Go back, ol' buggah, you sha'n't have dis boy.

He ain't no tramp, ner no straggler, of co'se;

He's pappy's pa'dner an' playmate an' joy.

Come to you' pallet now—go to yo' res';

Wisht you could allus know

　　ease an' cleah skies;

Wisht you could stay

　　jes' a chile on my

　　breas'—

Little brown baby wif

　　spa'klin' eyes!

SYMPATHY

This poem, written in standard English by Dunbar in 1900, is often thought to be about the hardships of being black in America during segregation. But though it can certainly be interpreted that way, Dunbar wrote it when he had tuberculosis—at a time when there was no cure for the disease. And so it is literally about how horrible it felt to be trapped inside a sick and dying body. Dunbar died in 1906 at the age of thirty-four.

I know what the caged bird feels, alas!

When the sun is bright on the upland slopes;

When the wind stirs soft through the springing grass,

And the river flows like a stream of glass;

When the first bird sings and the first bud opes,

And the faint perfume from its chalice steals—

I know what the caged bird feels!

I know why the caged bird beats his wing

Till its blood is red on the cruel bars;

For he must fly back to his perch and cling

When he fain would be on the bough a-swing;

And a pain still throbs in the old, old scars

And they pulse again with a keener sting—

I know why he beats his wing!

I know why the caged bird sings, ah me,

When his wing is bruised and his bosom sore,—

When he beats his bars and he would be free;

It is not a carol of joy or glee,

But a prayer that he sends from his heart's deep core,

But a plea, that upward to Heaven he flings—

I know why the caged bird sings!

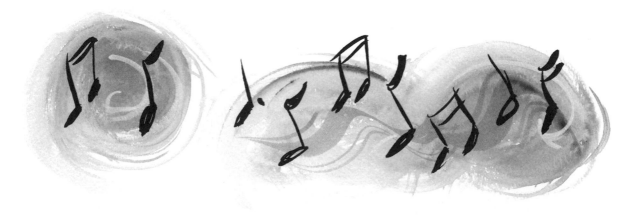

THE SAND-MAN

I know a man
With face of tan,
But who is ever kind;
Whom girls and boys
Leave games and toys
Each eventide to find.

When day grows dim,
They watch for him,
He comes to place his claim;
He wears the crown
Of Dreaming-town;
The sand-man is his name.

When sparkling eyes
Troop sleepywise
And busy lips grow dumb;
When little heads
Nod toward the beds,
We know the sand-man's come.

JAMES WELDON JOHNSON (1871–1938)

James Weldon Johnson, one of the leading figures of the Harlem Renaissance, was greatly influenced by Paul Laurence Dunbar. Born on June 17, 1871, in Jacksonville, Florida, Johnson was the first African American to pass the Florida bar examination, a test that enabled him to practice law. Instead, he chose to pursue a career in music and literature, and he and his brother, Rosamond, moved to New York in 1901 to work in musical theater. He published hundreds of stories and poems during his lifetime and became the first African American professor at New York University. He died in a car accident at the age of sixty-seven.

THE CREATION

One of Johnson's best-known works is God's Trombones: Seven Negro Sermons in Verse. *Published in 1927, it is a series of narrative poems based on African American folk sermons and includes "The Creation," which I performed at age fourteen at the Elk Oratorical Contest in Minneapolis in 1959.*

And God stepped out on space,

And He looked around and said,

"I'm lonely—

I'll make me a world."

And as far as the eye of God could see

Darkness covered everything,

Blacker than a hundred midnights

Down in a cypress swamp.

Then God smiled,

And the light broke,

And the darkness rolled up on one side,

And the light stood shining on the other,

And God said, *"That's good!"*

Then God reached out and took the light in His hands,

And God rolled the light around in His hands

Until He made the sun;

And He set that sun a-blazing in the heavens.

And the light that was left from making the sun

God gathered it up in a shining ball

And flung it against the darkness,

Spangling the night with the moon and stars.

Then down between

The darkness and the light

He hurled the world;

And God said, *"That's good!"*

Then God himself stepped down—

And the Sun was on his right hand,

And the Moon was on His left;

The stars were clustered about His head,

And the earth was under His feet.

And God walked, and where He trod

His footsteps hollowed the valleys out

And bulged the mountains up.

Then He stopped and looked and saw

That the earth was hot and barren.

So God stepped over to the edge of the world

And He spat out the seven seas;

He batted His eyes, and the lightnings flashed;

He clapped His hands, and the thunders rolled;

And the waters above the earth came down,

The cooling waters came down.

Then the green grass sprouted,

And the little red flowers blossomed,

The pine tree pointed his finger to the sky,

And the oak spread out his arms,

The lakes cuddled down in the hollows of the ground,

And the rivers ran down to the sea;

And God smiled again,

And the rainbow appeared,

And curled itself around His shoulder.

Then God raised His arm and He waved His hand

Over the sea and over the land,

And He said, *"Bring forth! Bring forth!"*

And quicker than God could drop His hand,

Fishes and fowls

And beasts and birds

Swam the rivers and the seas,

Roamed the forests and the woods,

And split the air with their wings.

And God said, *"That's good!"*

Then God walked around,

And God looked around

On all that He had made.

He looked at His sun,

And He looked at His moon,

And He looked at His little stars;

He looked on His world

With all its living things,

And God said, *"I'm lonely still."*

Then God sat down

On the side of a hill where He could think;

By a deep, wide river He sat down;

With His head in His hands,

God thought and thought,

Till He thought, *"I'll make me a man!"*

Up from the bed of the river

God scooped the clay;

And by the bank of the river

He kneeled Him down;

And there the Great God Almighty,

Who lit the sun and fixed it in the sky,

Who flung the stars to the most far corner of the night,

Who rounded the earth in the middle of His hand—

This Great God,

Like a mammy bending over her baby,

Kneeled down in the dust

Toiling over a lump of clay

Till He shaped it in His own image;

Then into it He blew the breath of life,

And man became a living soul.

Amen. Amen.

LIFT EV'RY VOICE AND SING

This song was written by Johnson and scored by his brother, Rosamond, in February 1900 to celebrate the 100th anniversary of the birth of Abraham Lincoln. It was first performed by 500 students at a black high school in Jacksonville, Florida, where Johnson was the principal.

The NAACP, founded in 1909, made "Lift Ev'ry Voice and Sing" its organizational anthem. (Johnson was chosen as a chief executive of the organization in 1920.) Soon the song was adopted by the entire African American community as "The Negro National Anthem," and it is still sung at many programs where black people gather.

Lift ev'ry voice and sing,

Till earth and heaven ring,

Ring with the harmonies of Liberty;

Let our rejoicing rise

High as the list'ning skies,

Let it resound loud as the rolling sea.

Sing a song full of the faith that the dark past has taught us,

Sing a song full of the hope that the present has brought us;

Facing the rising sun of our new day begun,

Let us march on till victory is won.

Stony the road we trod,

Bitter the chast'ning rod,

Felt in the days when hope unborn had died;

Yet with a steady beat,

Have not our weary feet

Come to the place for which our fathers sighed?

We have come over a way that with tears has been watered.

We have come, treading our path through the blood of the

    slaughtered,

Out from the gloomy past,

Till now we stand at last

Where the white gleam of our bright star is cast.

God of our weary years,

God of our silent tears,

Thou who hast brought us thus far on the way;

Thou who hast by Thy might

Led us into the light,

Keep us forever in the path, we pray.

Lest our feet stray from the places, our God, where we

    met Thee,

Lest our hearts, drunk with the wine of the world,

    we forget Thee;

Shadowed beneath Thy hand,

May we forever stand,

True to our God,

True to our native land.

LANGSTON HUGHES (1902–1967)

Langston Hughes grew up in Missouri, worked on a ship, and eventually earned a bachelor's degree from Lincoln University in Pennsylvania. He lived the majority of his adult life at 20 East 127th Street in Harlem. For forty years he was one of the most prolific and popular writers in the country, leaving a legacy that includes award-winning poetry, novels, plays, essays, and articles.

Hughes said he was inspired to write his first poem, "The Negro Speaks of Rivers," at age seventeen when he was crossing the Mississippi River on his way to visit his father in Mexico. Since then, Hughes's works have been critically acclaimed and credited with having a distinctive voice that is honest and easy to read, yet deep in meaning and clearly influenced by his love of jazz. Hughes always made his point with pride and dignity.

THE NEGRO SPEAKS OF RIVERS

I've known rivers:

I've known rivers ancient as the world and older than the

    flow of human blood in human veins.

My soul has grown deep like the rivers.

I bathed in the Euphrates when dawns were young.

I built my hut near the Congo and it lulled me to sleep.

I looked upon the Nile and raised the pyramids above it.

I heard the singing of the Mississippi when Abe Lincoln

    went down to New Orleans, and I've seen its muddy

    bosom turn all golden in the sunset.

I've known rivers:

Ancient, dusky rivers.

My soul has grown deep like the rivers.

I, TOO

"I, Too" can be read as a summary of Hughes's writing philosophy. It was published in 1945, ten years or so before the beginning of the civil rights movement, of which he became an outspoken part.

I, too, sing America.

I am the darker brother.

They send me to eat in the kitchen

When company comes,

But I laugh,

And eat well,

And grow strong.

Tomorrow,

I'll be at the table

When company comes.

Nobody'll dare

Say to me,

"Eat in the kitchen,"

Then.

Besides,

They'll see how beautiful I am

And be ashamed—

I, too, am America.

Chapter 9

ON THE PORCH OR BY THE FIRE
FOLKTALES AND STORYTELLING

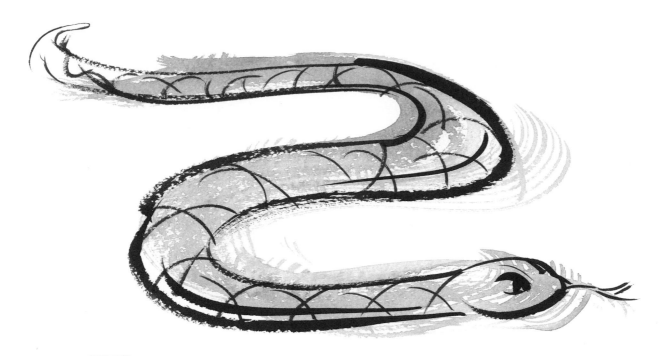

The spreading out of African people and their language and culture all around the world is called the African diaspora. *Diaspora* comes from the Greek word for dispersion, which means scattering.

Our ancestors brought to the Americas a treasure trove of wonderful stories, some fictional and others based on the lives of real people. Characters like Anansi the Spider and Zomo the Hare traveled from West Africa to their new Caribbean homes. Over time, the African characters merged with Caribbean and Native American characters and were renamed Aunt Nancy, Ti Malice, Br'er Rabbit, and later Bugs Bunny.

We loved a good yarn in my family, and it was a rite of passage to be invited to tell a story on the front porch or by the fireplace at my grandparents' house. In my mind, there was no room for failure, so I spent time choosing a tale that was entertaining and enlightening. I'd practice by telling it to my friends first. Then, if I was called upon to perform for adults, I was ready.

Later, when I became a teacher, I shared scary stories, tall tales, myths, and legends with my students. The ones they enjoyed most were the personal yarns about my ancestors. As a mother and grandmother, I shared these same stories with my young sons and grandchildren. I've selected a few to share with you.

ALL STORIES BELONG TO ANANSI
Retold by Patricia C. McKissack

African Anansi the spider stories are sometimes clever and smart, but at other times, Anansi is pathetically foolish.

His dual nature helps illustrate to listeners what is acceptable behavior, and the consequences of doing the contrary. The following is an original Anansi tale from the Akan people of West Africa.

All stories are said to be owned by Anansi the Spider. Here is how that came to be.

One day, Anansi went to the sky god, Nyame, and said, "I want to buy all the stories that are told now and forever."

Nyame answered, "Fine. But you must pay a high fee. Many great people have tried to pay me but failed. Do you really think you have a chance?"

"Name your price," Anansi answered confidently.

Nyame began, "First, I want Mmoboro the Hornets, who will make me shrewd and cunning. Next, I must have Onini the Python, who will grant me great strength, and finally, the fur of Osebo the Leopard, which will make me feared and respected. For these three things, I will sell you all stories."

"I can do that," bragged Anansi. And off he went to accomplish his first chore.

First, he cut a large gourd from a vine and bored a hole in it. Then he found a jug—also known as a calabash— filled it with water, and went to the tree where the hornets lived. Anansi dumped water over his head until he was dripping wet; then, without their noticing him, he poured water on the hive until it, too, was all wet, along with the hornets inside.

The hornets looked out and saw Anansi and figured it was raining. "Where can we go to get dry?" they asked.

Anansi told them to move into the gourd he had hung on a nearby branch of the tree. The unsuspecting hornets flew into the gourd, and quickly Anansi plugged up the hole. Then off he went to Nyame.

"You still have two more to bring," said the sky god.

Now Anansi cut an extra-long bamboo pole and went to the hole where it was said the great snake, Onini, lived. Anansi began to talk out loud, as if speaking to himself. "I think she is wrong. He is the strongest, the longest, and the smartest snake in the jungle." Then he repeated this, even louder.

"What are you saying, Anansi?" the python hissed.

In a manner that showed no fear, Anansi approached Onini and explained, "Well, my wife said you are not the strongest, the longest, or the smartest snake in the jungle. But I think you are."

"You are wise, Anansi. I am long enough and strong enough to wrap myself around an elephant and bring him down." The snake went on bragging about his abilities.

"You are a wonder!" shouted Anansi, heaping on all the flattery he could.

Then Anansi asked Onini, "May I measure you, so that I can tell my wife just how long you really are?"

"Why, of course," said Onini.

Anansi put the measuring pole down and Onini began stretching himself to reach the full length of the stick. Onini was still about a foot from the end, so he stretched and stretched. Finally, when the snake was weak from pushing and straining, harder and harder, the cunning spider rushed out and tied Onini to the pole. "My wife was wrong about two things—you are long, you are strong," said Anansi. "But she was right about one thing. You are not that smart." Then he stuffed the snake into a sack made of water buffalo hide and took him to Nyame.

Anansi had one more task to accomplish. He dug a deep hole and covered it with brush. Then he tied a rope around a tree branch and pulled it down and over the hole. Nothing now to do but wait.

Before long, Osebo the Leopard came bounding down the road. And as Anansi had planned, the big cat fell into the hole. Anansi called out to the leopard, "Grab hold of the tree limb and pull yourself up."

The leopard did as Anansi suggested, although he was furious. "I am going to devour the person who set this trap when I get out of here!" he shouted.

Oh, really, thought Anansi, and he cut the rope holding the tree branch. It whipped upright, hurling Osebo the Leopard out of the hole and high into the air.

Anansi killed Osebo, skinned him, and took the hide to Nyame. The sky god was amazed and pleased. He announced, "Kwaku Anansi (Uncle Anansi), you have done what mighty hunters, warriors, counselors, and kings have not been able to accomplish. So from this day forward, all stories belong to you!"

BR'ER RABBIT AND BR'ER FOX
Retold by Patricia C. McKissack

Slaves who were taken from the Hausa people of West Africa to the plantation South brought stories about Zomo the Hare, another trickster, who would become Br'er (Brother) Rabbit.

Joel Chandler Harris (1845–1908) was a white man who grew up hearing Br'er Rabbit tales told by the slaves who lived on the Georgia plantation where he worked. In the 1870s, he wrote down the tales he remembered and published them in the Atlanta Constitution, *the newspaper where he was a reporter.*

Unfortunately, Uncle Remus fit all the stereotypes whites had created about people of color. For African Americans, the problem was not with the stories Uncle Remus told, but with the historically inaccurate language patterns Harris gave him, filled with foolish representations of black speech and conduct. Here is a version written with more accurate language usage.

Br'er Fox decided to plant a garden with all kinds of good things to eat—sweet potatoes, squash, peas, and turnip greens. Yum! When the vegetables got up some size, Br'er Rabbit came along and spied the fresh goodies, just sittin' there waiting to be taken.

Br'er Rabbit ran home, got his wife and all six kids, and took them back to Br'er Fox's garden. They slipped under the fence and proceeded to fill their bellies full of the vegetables. This went on for a few days, until Br'er Fox noticed that his garden was being raided.

'Bout that time, Br'er Rabbit happened by. "My, my," he said, acting all surprised. "Looks like somebody's been stealing your vegetables."

"It do, don't it. I wonder who it might be," Br'er Fox replied, all the time spying a piece of carrot stuck in the rabbit's fur.

Now, Br'er Fox had a good idea of who the thief might be, but he couldn't prove it. So the fox, who was also a

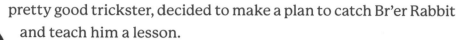

pretty good trickster, decided to make a plan to catch Br'er Rabbit and teach him a lesson.

First, Br'er Fox dug a deep hole at the gate of his garden and covered it with brush. Then he tied a rope around a long tree branch and pulled it over the hole. Then he tied another rope to the top of the tree branch and let the other rope end hang loosely over the hidden hole. Nothing now to do but wait.

And sure enough, here come Br'er Rabbit, steppin' lively. Just as he slipped under the gate, he tumbled headfirst into the hole. Br'er Rabbit was still wobbly-legged after falling in. And now Br'er Fox was hollering down at him.

"I gotcha, thief!" the fox shouted. "Gotcha."

"Let me out of here," the rabbit shouted back. "How dare you do this to me?"

"My, my, you're full of vinegar," Br'er Fox said, laughing. "You aine in no position to be daring anybody."

Br'er Rabbit sat down in a huff. Then he saw the rope hanging into the hole. He grabbed the rope, tied it to his back leg, and began climbing out. With each step he went on and on 'bout what he was going to do to Br'er Fox. But just when Br'er Rabbit had almost reached the top, the fox cut the rope that was holding the tree branch. The limb snapped upward, pulling Br'er Rabbit out of the hole upside down.

Br'er Fox rolled over laughing. Neighbors came to see what all the commotion was about. When they saw Br'er Rabbit swinging upside down from a tree branch, they laughed, too. Then, in front of all their friends, Br'er Fox gave Br'er Rabbit an ultimatum. "I'll let you go if you'll confess that you're a thief."

Come nightfall, Br'er Rabbit hadn't uttered a word. He just hung there. One by one everybody went home; they had better things to do than wait for Br'er Rabbit to admit to something everybody knew anyway.

So in the end it was just Br'er Fox and Br'er Rabbit. "I ought to skin you," said Br'er Fox.

"Or you could call it a draw and cut me loose," said Br'er Rabbit.

And that's what happened.

THREE CAUTIONARY TALES

The following three folktales have the same theme: "Beware of talking too much." They are cautionary tales, meant to warn listeners, and are examples of the way ideas are transferred from culture to culture through story sharing.

THE SKULL

Retold by Patricia C. McKissack

This story is from Nigerian West Africa.

A hunter returning from a hunt came upon a skull on the side of the road. "How are you, sir?" the skull asked respectfully.

"You . . . you . . . you spoke to me," sputtered the hunter. He looked around to see if someone could verify that an actual skull had spoken. There was no one nearby. After collecting his courage, he asked the skull, "What brought you here?"

"Beware!" the skull moaned. "Talk put me here; it will put you here, too."

But the hunter wasn't interested in the skull's warning, and he hurried to the village to tell the king what had happened. "There is a talking skull on the side of the road. It greeted me!" the hunter cried.

The king leaned forward with interest. "I've never heard of a talking skull," he said. "I want to see such a thing. Take me to it immediately."

The hunter led the king and his party to the skull. "Speak to me," the king demanded.

But the skull didn't speak.

The king snapped his demand again. When the skull refused to answer, the king told the hunter, "You unlock the skull's mouth or your head will rest beside his."

The hunter begged and pleaded with the skull to say something—anything! But sadly, it just sat there lifeless, never uttering a single word. The king ordered his guards to kill the hunter and leave his head beside the silent skull.

After the guards had done so, the group left.

After a time, the hunter's head gave a big sigh. "You were right. Talking too much brought you to this place, and talking has brought me here, too."

THE SINGING TORTOISE

Retold by Patricia C. McKissack

This story is from Haiti.

Haiti was one of the main slave ports and markets in the Caribbean. The slaves came from many parts of Africa, and so did their languages, customs, and beliefs; consequently, their shared stories reflect a variety of African cultures. This Haitian tale features a character associated with Anansi, named Ti Malice. Like the African character, Ti Malice is known for talking too much and for not being very truthful—a ne'er-do-well rascal.

A man, we shall call him Ti Malice, was known all over the island for talking too much. He always began his stories with "Would I tell you a word of a lie?" Everybody knew the answer was *yes,* no doubt about it. For Ti Malice the question should have been, "Have I ever spoken the truth?"

Ti Malice was down by the shore fishing when he saw a tortoise. When she reached Ti Malice, she started to sing.

> *Birds have beautiful feathers.*
> *How bright and colorful they are.*
> *Oh, if I had lovely feathers,*
> *Then I would fly away far.*

Ti Malice enjoyed the tortoise's song, and he asked her to come closer and sing to him again.

The Tortoise was trusting and had no fear, until Ti Malice grabbed her and stuffed her into his fishing bag.

"I'm a rich man now!" he boasted as he hurried home.

There he hid the tortoise, put on his best clothes, and went off to tell his neighbors at the market what he had found.

"I have a singing tortoise," he announced to all those who were in the square.

"What is this you say?" said one merchant.

"There he goes again with one of his tales of no truth," said another.

"Every word is just as I say. I have a singing tortoise! And I will prove it, but you've got to pay first."

146

"I've never seen Ti Malice display such confidence," said another merchant. "He might be telling the—"

"Stop! He is tricking you!" shouted the seller of cabbages. "Ti Malice doesn't have a singing tortoise. I'll take that bet he's offering."

"I will, too!" cried still another merchant.

The bets came faster now. Ti Malice couldn't have been happier. At last the crowd caught the attention of the chief of police. "What you up to now, Ti Malice? No good, I'm sure!"

"He claims to have a singing tortoise. Who ever heard of such?" someone yelled.

"Is this what you've been telling the people?" asked the officer.

"I have, because it is true," answered Ti Malice.

"Show it to me," ordered the officer.

"You must pay like all the rest," Ti Malice said boldly. But he wouldn't have been so outspoken if he'd known what was happening back at his house.

In Ti Malice's hut, his wife was determined to find out what her husband had brought home. She found his fishing sack and looked inside. There she found the tortoise.

"What is this?" she said, taking the creature out. Figuring the tortoise couldn't be the cause of her husband's excitement, Mrs. Malice opened the door and turned her loose.

"Go, Tortoise. Live free!"

The tortoise was so happy, she began singing joyfully:

Birds have beautiful feathers.
How bright and colorful they are.
Oh, if I had lovely feathers,
Then I would fly away far.

Now birds of all kinds came, lifted the tortoise up, and flew her to safety.

Instantly, Mrs. Malice thought she might have done something wrong. She hurried to find her husband.

By the time she reached Ti Malice, the chief of police had him by the collar and was yelling, "Unless you can show us a singing tortoise, I will throw you in jail, where they'll give you a good beating. You'll remember the next time you form your mouth to speak a lie."

"You're going to beg my pardon when this is all said and done," Ti Malice said, laughing. "All of you are going to be amazed!"

Mrs. Malice knew now the mistake she had made freeing the tortoise. She tried to stop her husband from talking, but he wouldn't shut up! At last she found a moment, and she pulled him aside and whispered what she had done. "I am so, so sorry," she said sadly.

"You have made an end to me," wailed Ti Malice. "Oh, woe upon my head!"

"Show us the singing tortoise!" the people began to chant. "Show us the singing tortoise!"

Ti Malice didn't know what to do.

Mrs. Malice stepped up to defend her husband. "There really was a tortoise. By mistake, I found her and let her go free. As soon as I did, the critter began to sing and birds came and flew away with her."

The crowd fell silent. Fortunately, Mrs. Malice was known for being a kind and honest person in the marketplace where she sold her fresh vegetables. But still, she was married to Ti Malice, the worst scroundrel on the island.

"Mrs. Malice," said the chief of police calmly. "How do we know you are not repeating the lie your husband told? Or perhaps you are trying to save him from a beating he might not survive."

"No matter! Let's off with them to the jail, where we'll skin them both with a whip," someone in the crowd shouted. "Now!"

Just then a flock of birds flew overhead. They were carrying a tortoise.

And the tortoise was singing:

> *True! Ti Malice is a rascal.*
> *But who's better than his wife?*
> *Ti Malice is a ne'er-do-well,*
> *But Mrs. Malice saved my life.*
> *Mrs. Malice gave me freedom;*
> *Her kindness must be rewarded.*
> *I'm not singing to save Malice,*

But yes, it is as they recorded.
Birds have beautiful feathers.
How bright and colorful they are.
Oh, if I had lovely feathers,
Then I would fly away far.

The birds lifted the singing tortoise higher and flew away with her. The couple was freed at once. To everybody's dismay, they had to pay their bets, and indeed, the chief of police had to beg Ti Malice's pardon.

"I was wrong. I am sorry, Ti Malice," the officer said. "But I doubly apologize to you, Mrs. Malice," he added, turning to her respectfully. "You are a good woman, but this husband and that mouth of his is going to eventually make an end to you both."

JOHN, MASSA, AND CHARLIE THE MULE

Retold by Patricia C. McKissack

This final cautionary tale was told in the plantation South. Ol' John was a trickster, much like Anansi, but his single purpose was to foil his master's plans and make him look foolish.

One day, John rose early and went to the barn to hitch up ol' Charlie. The mule was slower than usual and more stubborn—plain mean! John lost his patience and gave Charlie a good whack 'cross his backside with a switch.

Hee-haw, hee-haw, complained the mule, but he still didn't move.

John took a whip this time and whacked Charlie again.

"Ouch!" shouted the mule. "That hurt!"

John looked around, shocked and confused. "Who said that?"

Charlie was quiet. John looked at the mule and told himself, "I aine crazy; mules can't talk."

After he had convinced himself of that fact, John tried to pull Charlie toward the fields. There was plenty of work to do, and John wanted to get ahead of the noonday sun, before it got double-hot with no breeze stirrin' at all. Mercy. "I say, let's go, ol' mule," he ordered.

"I don't wanna! And I'm gon' tell Massa 'bout you sleeping under the big maple tree half the day, and how you beat me, and call me names. . . ."

John jumped away from Charlie like he had stuck his hand in fire. And he ran toward the Big House.

Massa saw John a-comin'. "Where you going in such a hurry?" he asked.

"I aine working with no mule what talks." And John folded his arms and refused to go near Charlie.

"You say this old mule talked to you?" Massa asked, raising an eyebrow.

"Same as you talking to me." Then, moving right along, John dug the hole a little deeper. "And if that ol' rascal should tell you that I sleep half the day, and beat him unfairly, don't believe him. He's lying!"

Massa walked over to the mule. "Ummm! Did you talk to John?"

Charlie, he don't say nothing.

Massa asked once mo' and again. "Did you talk to John?"

Mule still don't say nothing.

Massa studied John's expression. "You still say he talked to you?"

"Yes, sir," said John. "Say something, Charlie, please!"

Charlie aine spoke yet. Never a word. Not one.

The rest of the day John had to work the field in the hot, hot sun without the help of the mule. Massa gave Charlie the day off, which he spent resting under the maple tree where John slept most days.

Back at the mansion, Massa chuckled. "John really thought I'd believe his tale," he said, adding, "Everybody knows a mule can't talk."

"Most intelligent people do, for sure," said the yellow dog that followed ol' Massa everywhere. "But John's a slave; he aine smart as you."

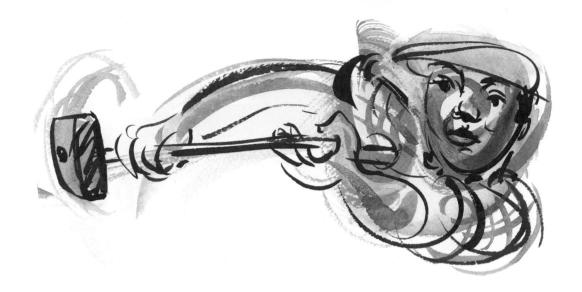

THE BALLAD OF JOHN HENRY, A STEEL-DRIVING MAN

John Henry is an African American folk hero created in the nineteenth century, a legendary character who worked building the railroad. His job was to hammer steel drills into rock to make holes for explosives that would clear the way for a tunnel. When the debris was removed, rails could be laid for the tracks. In actuality, this process took a lot of hard work by thousands of underpaid laborers—whites, Asians, and African Americans.

An African American railroad worker named John Henry actually lived. But his life story is lost, and it is hard to separate the facts from the fiction. Still, one thing is certain: John Henry represented working-class men who were competing with machines for their jobs. And he stands tall among America's other folk legends—Paul Bunyan, Pecos Bill, and Casey at the Bat. But to African Americans, John Henry was an icon who symbolized not just physical strength and hard work with dignity, but racial pride and solidarity.

My grandfather Daddy James introduced John Henry to me. We called him the Hammer Man. Like John Henry, my grandfather was a laborer who understood hard work for little pay. As a master storyteller, Daddy James combined fact and fiction to create a John Henry who was special to us.

Here is a version of the John Henry legend close to the one I remember hearing. It was told in the form of a ballad. Storytellers recited the long narrative poem, usually accompanying it with a guitar, a drum, a harmonica, or rhythmic hand clapping, as my grandfather did.

When John Henry was a little tiny baby

Sitting on his mama's knee,

He picked up a hammer and a little piece of steel,

153

Saying, "Hammer's going to be the death of me, Lord, Lord,

Hammer's going to be the death of me."

John Henry was a man just six feet high,

Nearly two feet and a half across his breast.

He'd hammer with a nine-pound hammer all day

And never get tired and want to rest, Lord, Lord,

And never get tired and want to rest.

John Henry went up on the mountain

And he looked one eye straight up its side.

The mountain was so tall and John Henry was so small,

He laid down his hammer and he cried, "Lord, Lord,"

He laid down his hammer and he cried.

John Henry said to his captain,

"Captain, you go to town,

Bring me back a *twelve*-pound

   hammer, please,

And I'll beat that steam drill down,

   Lord, Lord,

      I'll beat that steam

      drill down."

The captain said to John Henry,

"I believe this mountain's sinking in."

But John Henry said, "Captain, just you stand aside—

It's nothing but my hammer catching wind, Lord, Lord,

      It's nothing but my hammer catching wind."

John Henry said to his shaker,

"Shaker, boy, you better start to pray,

'Cause if my *twelve*-pound hammer miss that little piece of steel,

Tomorrow'll be your burying day, Lord, Lord,

      Tomorrow'll be your burying day."

John Henry said to his captain,

"A man is nothing but a man,

But before I let your steam drill beat me down,

I'd die with a hammer in my hand, Lord, Lord,

I'd die with a hammer in my hand."

The man that invented the steam drill,

He figured he was mighty high and fine,

But John Henry sunk the steel down fourteen feet

While the steam drill only made nine, Lord, Lord,

The steam drill only made nine.

John Henry hammered on the right-hand side.

Steam drill kept driving on the left.

John Henry beat that steam drill down.

But he hammered his poor heart to death, Lord, Lord,

He hammered his poor heart to death.

Well, they carried John Henry down the tunnel

And they laid his body in the sand.

Now every woman riding on a C and O train

Says, "There lies my steel-driving man, Lord, Lord,

There lies my steel-driving man."

LAUGHING LIZZY—A JUMP TALE

Written by Patricia C. McKissack for this collection

One of the most requested genres in the lexicon of African American oral tradition is the scary story. In the South, every town, large or small, had its resident ghost. For those who lived in Briarsville, Tennessee, a black community a few miles outside Nashville, the local terror was a spirit named Laughing Lizzy. When my grandmother Mama Frances told this tale in the dark of a summer night, we kids would huddle together, frightened yet excited. This story has another feature that I will share later, so as not to spoil the surprise. Meanwhile, I will retell "Laughing Lizzy" as I remember hearing it back in 1954. Happy horrors!

Elizabeth came to Briarsville from up east somewhere and never left, because she met and married Adam within the year of her arrival. She was a beautiful young bride with an infectious laugh and happy, sparkling eyes. Adam lovingly called her his Laughing Lizzy.

The couple built a little house in a clearing in the woods and filled it with the joyful sounds of children—two girls and two boys.

Then one awful night, there was a fire that destroyed it all. The little house, Adam, the children—the whole family—died, all save Lizzy. She had run into the blazing house to save at least one of them, but she had failed and now was horribly burned and disfigured. It was more than she could endure, and she began hysterically laughing. It wasn't a sound of joy or glee, but a high-pitched, shrill scream of madness.

There were no places for people like Lizzy to get help in that long-ago time, so neighbors took turns caring for her, making sure her needs were met. Lizzy's physical wounds healed in time, but her mental scars remained fresh and painful. Some nights she would wander down to the clearing where the chimney of her burned-out house still stood, and the neighbors would find her there, pathetically pressing a log to her breast as if it were one of her children. And when they'd try to take her away, she would begin her terrible laughing, which grew louder, and even louder, until she was screaming and wailing in anguish!

When it was her time, Lizzy died. But the residents of Briarsville say her laughter lived on. Hunters passing by the crumbling, vine-covered chimney claimed they heard Lizzy and fled in fear. And soon the sound of her woeful laughter rising on the night winds became an omen of some tragedy to visit whoever had heard her. People covered their ears and those of their children to avoid hearing Laughing Lizzy!

At this point Mama Frances finished the story. We were mesmerized, sitting stone still and quiet. Then my grandmother would throw back her head and in a very loud, high-pitched, and shrill voice laugh:

"Ha-ha, ha, ha, ha, ha!!!!!!
"Gotcha!"

This ending, of course, causes unsuspecting listeners to jump—and works best when the listeners aren't ready for the surprise. Jump tale endings usually enhance a good scary story. Two favorite scary stories or jump tales my sons enjoyed while growing up were "Wiley and the Hairy Man" and "I Want My Liver Back!" Look them up and be ready to tell them on a dark and moonless night.

ACKNOWLEDGMENTS

Writing this book has been an adventure that led me down the rabbit hole to a wonderland of imagination and surprise. The Alice in me rejoiced in meeting the many people who helped me rediscover the games, songs, and stories I enjoyed as a child and that are included in this collection. I owe a huge debt of gratitude to those who helped with this project. A special thanks to the boys and girls in more than twelve states who allowed me to "play" with them at camps; in public, private, and parochial schools; in Sunday schools of all denominations; and in parks and libraries.

The help I received from Patti Carlton, children's librarian at the St. Louis Central Library, and also from the staff of St. Louis County Library branches, was immeasurable.

I appreciate Dr. Brenda Fyfe, dean of the School of Education, Webster University, St. Louis, for pointing me in the right direction. Thank you to Dr. Rudine Sims-Bishop, former professor of Library Science at Ohio State University, for all her helpful suggestions and comments.

My three sons and five grandchildren have helped me in ways that are too numerous to list. My sister, Sarah Stuart, who played these games, sang these songs, and heard the same stories I did, made many comments and ideas I used joyfully. Thanks to Onawumi Jean Moss, Linda Goss, and members of the storytelling community for all their support and input. Fredrick L. McKissack, my husband and partner, did most of the research for this book before his death in April 2013, and there are those, perhaps, who helped him without my knowledge. If that is the case, I thank you for anything you or your organization contributed to this process.

A very special shout-out to Brian Pinkney, whose brilliant artwork added color and movement to our playful world.

Finally, this book would have remained an idea if not for the efforts of my editor, Anne Schwartz, and the rest of the wonderful crew at Schwartz & Wade—Stephanie Pitts, Lee Wade, Rachael Cole, and Annie Kelley. Thank you.

NOTES

Chapter 1
FROM HAND TO HAND
Hand Claps

Patty-Cake: This hand clap rhyme, known originally as "Pat-a-Cake," originated in England. The earliest recorded version appears in the 1698 play *The Campaigners,* written by Thomas D'Urfey.

Solomon Grundy: This rhyme was collected by James Halliwell and published in London in 1842. It arrived in the United States with immigrants and entered the larger American culture. The All-American Comics Company featured a character called Solomon Grundy in its series of heroes in October 1944. The cartoon character should not be confused with the old English rhyme. They are two separate entities.

Eenie Meenie Miney Mo: In 1902 the pejorative racial rhyme was used in the chorus of a song by Bert Fitzgibbons, "Eenie, Meany, Miny Mo." Then Rudyard Kipling used the pejorative version in his *Land and Sea Tales for Scouts and Guides,* published in 1923. By the 1940s the hand clap rhyme was scorned by most African Americans.

Shimmy, Shimmy Coco Pop: The rapper Nelly used a variation of the Little Anthony song in his Country Grammar album. He altered the phrase "Shimmy, shimmy ko-ko bop" to "Shimmy, shimmy coco pop/pow" and created a new version of the familiar rhyme.

Chapter 2
TURN ABOUT
Jump Rope Rhymes and Games

Tug-of-War: From 1900 to 1920, tug-of-war was included as an Olympic sport, but it was then dropped. Today the sport is part of the World Games. Men and women from fifty-three nations, including the United States, belong to TWIF (Tug of War International Federation).

Chapter 3
SHAKE YO' BODY
Circle Games and Ring Shouts

Little Sally (Waters) Walker: Wilma King wrote in her 1995 book, *Stolen Childhood*, that "Little Sally Waters" originated in the plantation South during the mid-nineteenth century.

The soul singer Rufus Thomas's R&B version of "Little Sally Walker" became popular in 1965—which reintroduced the chant to African American children.

Shake Your Body: Born in 1927, Harry Belafonte, an African American hero, rose to fame as a singer, songwriter, actor, and social activist during the 1950s and 1960s. He recorded the song "Jump in the Line (Shake, Señora)," based on a 1946 composition by Trinidadian Alwyn Roberts, better known as Lord Kitchener. Belafonte included the song on his 1961 album *Jump Up Calypso,* which became hugely successful.

He's Got the Whole World in His Hands: In 1958 an English singer, Laurie London, and the Geoff Love Orchestra took "He's Got the Whole World in His Hands" to number one on the popular charts and an amazing number three on the rhythm and blues (R&B) charts.

Since that time it has been recorded by many musicians, including Mahalia Jackson, Odetta, Nina Simone, Andy Williams, and Pat Boone.

Kum Bah Yah: "Kum Bah Yah" remained basically unknown outside the Gullah culture until Pete Seeger, a folk singer, recorded it in 1958, giving it new life. Black children all over the country made it a part of their circle games and used stomps to create a sound that imitated African drumming.

Chapter 4
FOLLOW THE DRINKING GOURD
Songs Inspired by the Underground Railroad

"Gourd" is an African term for cup.

Songs Using Coded Words: Members of the African Methodist Episcopal Church—founded by Richard Allen in Philadelphia in 1816—were leading advocates of the underground escape system. Among supporters of slavery, the AME Church was called the Abolitionist Church, and it was banned in most Southern states. However, this didn't keep members out of the struggle.

Steal Away: Wallis Willis, a Choctaw freedman living near Hugo, Oklahoma, was overheard singing "Steal Away" by Alexander Reid, a minister at the Old Spencer Academy, a Choctaw boarding school, in 1862. After the Civil War, Reid wrote down the music and lyrics he'd heard and sent it to the Jubilee Singers at Fisk University, where the song was identified as an old spiritual, inspired by the stories of the Jordan River and Elijah, who was taken to heaven in a fiery chariot (2 Kings 2:11). "Steal Away" is also categorized as a conductor's contact song used on the Underground Railroad.

Swing Low, Sweet Chariot: Araminta Harriet Ross (later Harriet Tubman) was born a slave in Dorchester, Maryland, around 1820. The exact date is unknown. During the Civil War Tubman served as a spy for the Union Army. She lived out the remainder of her life in upstate New York.

Chapter 5
MAKE A JOYFUL NOISE
Spirituals, Hymns, and Gospel Music

Spirituals: "Sometimes I Feel Like a Motherless Child" dates to the first half of the nineteenth century. It was recorded by Paul Robeson in 1925 and Mahalia Jackson in 1955.

Hymns: "In Praise of Aten" is one of the oldest hymns on record; it was written for the ancient Egyptian pharaoh Akhenaton. The "Homeric Hymns" were written in the seventh century BC and glorified Greek deities. By comparison, Christian hymns are relatively new; they can be traced to the first century AD. In the beginning they were chanted by the priests or sung a cappella (without instruments), but by the sixteenth century they were accompanied by a choir or the entire congregation. Today, hymns are a part of church services in many denominations.

Jesus Loves Me: This first appeared as a poem written by Anna Bartlett Warner in an 1860 novel by her sister, Susan Warner. It was set to music in 1862 by William Bradbury.

Jesus Loves the Little Children: This song was written by C. Herbert Woolston.

I'll Be a Sunbeam: Based on Judges 5:31, this song was written by Nellie Talbot in 1900 and set to music by Edwin O. Excell, who published it in his hymnal, *Praises,* in Chicago in 1905. "Jesus Wants Me for a Sunbeam," written in 1987 by the alternative rock band the Vaselines, is a parody of that song. The titles are often confused.

This Little Light of Mine: This was written by Avis Christiansen and scored by teacher and composer Harry Dixon Loes around 1920, based on Matthew 5:16.

Precious Lord, Take My Hand: Thomas Dorsey (1899–1993) was music director at Pilgrim Baptist Church in Chicago when he wrote "Precious Lord, Take My Hand." Well-known black and white vocalists performed it, and took gospel to the hearts and homes of people via radio and television, records, and concerts. Some religious leaders say this song made gospel music popular across many cultures and ushered it into the contemporary era.

I'll Fly Away: Words and music to "I'll Fly Away" were written in 1929 by Albert E. Brumley (1905–1977) and published in 1932 by Hartford Music Company.

Chapter 6
PEARLS OF WISDOM
Proverbs, Psalms, and Parables

The psalms and parables used in this chapter are based on those in the King James Bible.

The Twenty-Third Psalm: Psalm 23 can be found in the Old Testament of the Christian Bible.

The Parables of Jesus: The Parables of Jesus are stories he told during his ministry. There are forty-six parables in the New Testament Gospels of Matthew, Mark, and Luke. There are five parables in the Jewish Torah, and there are also Islamic, Hindu, and Buddhist parables.

The Mustard Seed: The parable of the mustard seed is so well known and well loved in the black community that African American children, during their confirmations or baptisms, are often given a glass-encased mustard seed on a necklace or bracelet to symbolize their hopes, dreams, wishes, and faith.

Chapter 7
A WORD TO THE WISE
Superstitions, Fables, and Mama Sayings

Superstitions: It is believed that superstitions grew out of real situations. Here's an example that dates back to nineteenth-century Virginia: Christmas trees that were set by the fireplace—which were usually blazing—often caught fire. After a while people began saying, "Don't place the Christmas tree next to the fireplace—it's bad luck." Once there was central heating and fireplaces weren't always lit, the "superstition" remained.

Aesop's Fables: Though none of his actual writings still exist, Aesop, belived to have been an Afro-Greek slave born around 620 BC, has been credited with writing an assortment of wonderful fables.

Historians have debated for centuries the details of Aesop's life. Some think he was a horribly deformed African slave, whose outstanding intellect earned him his freedom and a position as an adviser to kings. Still others argue that Aesop was a fictional character, featured in a Greek play. A few researchers have suggested that Aesop was in reality a group of people who collected stories under one name.

All of these fables have been retold by me, based on collections of Aesop's stories.

Chapter 8

ON PROGRAM

Performance Pieces Inspired by African American Writers

Paul Laurence Dunbar (1872–1906): Dunbar's work dates from 1880 to 1906.

James Weldon Johnson (1871–1938): Johnson also wrote *The Autobiography of an Ex-Colored Man,* published in 1927. He died June 26, 1938, in a car accident in Wiscasset, Maine.

Langston Hughes (1902–1967): This Harlem Renaissance writer lived in Joplin, Missouri, until he was thirteen. His many travels began when he moved with his mother and stepfather to Lincoln, Illinois, then later to Cleveland, Ohio. After he graduated from high school, Hughes moved to Mexico for a year. He moved again, this time to New York, to attend Columbia University from 1921 to 1922. Growing restless once again, he left school and got a job on a ship, where he served as a cook, and traveled to Africa and Europe.

Hughes's first poem, "The Negro Speaks of Rivers," was discovered by W. E. B. Du Bois, editor of *The Crisis* magazine, the publishing arm of the National Association for the Advancement of Colored People (NAACP), in 1921. "I, Too" is included in *The Collected Poems of Langston Hughes* (New York: Alfred A. Knopf, 1994).

After his death in 1967, Hughes's home became a historical landmark.

Chapter 9

ON THE PORCH OR BY THE FIRE

Folktales and Storytelling

I've retold the stories in this chapter based on a variety of resources, but the entries are my own interpretations.

The African Diaspora: To better understand the African diaspora, find a world map. Locate the nations on the west side of the continent of Africa. Use your finger to trace a direct ship route across the Atlantic Ocean to the island of Haiti. Then, leaving Haiti, pretend to sail north to the mouth of the Mississippi River or up the eastern coast of Florida, to Georgia, the Carolinas, Virginia, and all the way to New York. You've just followed one of the slave trade routes. Other routes took slaves from Africa to other islands in the Caribbean, to Brazil, and to Europe.

Br'er Rabbit and Br'er Fox: Though the wily rabbit has a direct link to Africa, there are Br'er Rabbit stories that are undeniably based on Cherokee lore as well. Among the French-speaking storytellers of Louisiana, Br'er Rabbit was renamed Compair Lapin, and among the Algonquin Indians of the northeastern United States, he was Nanabozho, the Trickster Hare.

Joel Chandler Harris was not the first to publish the Br'er Rabbit stories, but his collections were the most successful. Today these stories have made a comeback, rewritten by Julius Lester and illustrated by Jerry Pinkney. Their book *Uncle Remus: The Complete Tales* more accurately represents the language patterns and cultural history of the time and people.

The Ballad of John Henry, a Steel-Driving Man: John Henry emerged at a time when a black hero was needed. Between 1860 and 1900, machines were taking over many of the jobs men had held. For laborers, "the machine" was a sign of doom, a job-stealer that deprived them of an honest living. So when a brave young man with seemingly endless strength joined them, railroad workers both black and white celebrated his accomplishments and honored him.

John Henry inspired songs that have been recorded by Bruce Springsteen, Harry Belafonte, and others, as well as novels, plays, films, and poetry.

BIBLIOGRAPHY

Chapter 1
FROM HAND TO HAND
Hand Claps

Booker, M. Keith, ed. *The Encyclopedia of Comic Books and Graphic Novels,* 2 Vols. Santa Barbara, CA: Greenwood, 2010.

Carlisle, Rodney, ed. *Encyclopedia of Play in Today's Society,* 2 Vols. Thousand Oaks, CA: Sage Publications, 2009.

Gaunt, Kyra D. *The Games Black Girls Play: Learning the Ropes from Double-Dutch to Hip-Hop.* New York: New York University Press, 1998.

Opie, Iona, and Peter Opie, eds. *The Oxford Dictionary of Nursery Rhymes.* Oxford: Oxford University Press, 1997.

Chapter 2
TURN ABOUT
Jump Rope Rhymes and Games

Hawthorne, Ruth. "Classifying Jump-Rope Games." *Keystone Folklore Quarterly,* Vol. 11, Spring 1966.

Chapter 3
SHAKE YO' BODY
Circle Games and Ring Shouts

American Society of Composers, Authors and Publishers, online search, August 2014.

Billboard, Feb. 20, 1965.

Cross, Wilbur. *Gullah Culture in America.* Winston-Salem, NC: John F. Blair, 2008.

King, Wilma. *Stolen Childhood: Slave Youth in Nineteenth-Century America.* Bloomington: Indiana University Press, 1995.

Moore, James, Jr. *The Treasury of American Prayers.* New York: Doubleday, 2008.

Vaughan Williams Memorial Library, Anne Geddes Gilchrist Collection, online archive. August 2014.

Chapter 4
FOLLOW THE DRINKING GOURD
Songs Inspired by the Underground Railroad

Lowance, Mason, ed. *Against Slavery: An Abolitionist Reader.* New York: Penguin Books, 2000.

Tobin, Jacqueline L., and Raymond G. Dobard. *Hidden in Plain View: A Secret Story of Quilts and the Underground Railroad.* New York: Doubleday, 1999.

Chapter 5
MAKE A JOYFUL NOISE
Spirituals, Hymns, and Gospel Music

---

www.fisk.edu/about/history#1871

Graham, Patricia Kelsey. *We Shall Make Music: Stories of the Primary Songs and How They Came to Be.* Springville, UT: Cedar Fort, 2007.

Hoffelt, Robert O., and Vinton Randolph Anderson, eds. *The African Methodist Episcopal Church Bicentennial Hymnal.* Nashville, TN: AME Publishing Co., 1984.

O'Neal, Jim, and Amy van Singel, eds. *The Voice of the Blues: Classic Interviews from* Living Blues *Magazine.* New York: Routledge, 2012.

Solomon, Olivia and Jack, eds. *"Honey in the Rock": The Ruby Pickens Tartt Collection of Religious Folk Songs from Sumter County, Alabama.* Macon, Georgia: Mercer University Press, 1991.

Southern, Eileen. *The Music of Black Americans,* Second Edition, New York: W.W. Norton & Company, 1971.

Chapter 6
PEARLS OF WISDOM
Proverbs, Psalms, and Parables

Chenu, Bruno. *The Trouble I've Seen: The Big Book of Negro Spirituals.* Valley Forge, PA: Judson Press, 2003.

McMickle, Marvin A. *An Encyclopedia of African American Christian Heritage.* Valley Forge, PA: Judson Press, 2003.

Stewart, Julia. *African Proverbs and Wisdom.* Secaucus, New Jersey: Citadel Press, 1997.

Chapter 7
A WORD TO THE WISE
Superstitions, Fables, and Mama Sayings

Mishra, Ratit P., Andrea L. Stanton, Edward Ramsamy, Peter J. Seybolt, Carolyn M. Elliott, eds. *Cultural Sociology of the Middle East, Asia, and Africa: An Encyclopedia.* Thousand Oaks, CA: Sage Publishing, 2012.

Chapter 8
ON PROGRAM
Performance Pieces Inspired by African American Writers

Jackson, Kenneth T., and David S. Dunbar, eds. *Empire City: New York Through the Centuries.* New York: Columbia University Press, 2002.

Johnson, James Weldon. *The Essential Writings of James Weldon Johnson.* New York: Random House, 2011.

———, *God's Trombones.* New York: Viking, 1927.

McKissack, Patricia C. *Paul Laurence Dunbar: A Poet to Remember.* Chicago: Children's Press/Scholastic, 1984.

Peebles, James W., ed. *The Life and Works of Paul Laurence Dunbar.* Nashville, TN: Winston-Derek Publishers, Inc., 1992.

Rampersad, Arnold, and David Roessel, eds. *The Collected Poems of Langston Hughes.* New York: Vintage, 1995.

Randall, Dudley, ed. *The Black Poets.* New York: Bantam Books, 1971.

Socarides, Alexandria, "Poems (We Think) We Know: The Negro Speaks of Rivers," *Los Angeles Review of Books,* Aug. 1, 2013.

Chapter 9
ON THE PORCH OR BY THE FIRE
Folktales and Storytelling

Bascom, William W. *African Folktales in the New World.* Bloomington: Indiana University Press, 1976.

Bickley, R. Bruce, Jr. *Joel Chandler Harris: A Biography and Critical Study.* Athens, Georgia: University of Georgia Press, 2008.

Courlander, Harold. *A Treasury of African Folklore.* New York: Marlowe and Company, 1996.

———, *A Treasury of Afro-American Folklore.* New York: Marlowe and Company, 1976, 1996.

Lester, Julius. *Uncle Remus: The Complete Tales.* New York: Dial, 1999.

M'Baye, Babacar. *The Trickster Comes West: Pan-African Influence in Early Black Diasporan Narratives.* Jackson: University Press of Mississippi, 2009.

Nelson, Scott Reynolds, *Steel Drivin' Man: John Henry: The Untold Story of an American Legend.* New York: Oxford University Press, 2006.

COPYRIGHT ACKNOWLEDGMENTS

INDEX